It was driving him crazy.

She was driving him crazy.

Simon didn't know what was wrong with him. He couldn't seem to control the raw desire that grew stronger each time he and Jenny were together.

She was no longer the Jenny he knew.

He no longer felt comfortable with her.

He had liked her a lot better when she was just… Jenny. Feisty and fun and easy to be with.

Now he was afraid to be around her. Afraid he might do or say something to give away his strange new feelings.

Any time they were together, all he could think about was…

Simon swallowed. Hard.

Damn! He hated the way Jenny was changing!

Dear Reader,

Silhouette **Special Edition** welcomes you to romance…
and to summer! June is sure to be the start of a great season,
beginning, of course, with THAT SPECIAL WOMAN!
This month, bestselling author Sherryl Woods takes you
on a journey like you've never experienced…and neither
has her heroine, who gets into more trouble than she can
handle—but she *does* have a sexy adventurer by her side in
Riley's Sleeping Beauty.

June also marks the beginning of a wonderful new trilogy,
MAN, WOMAN AND CHILD, from veteran authors
Christine Flynn, Robin Elliott and Pat Warren. It all begins
this month with *A Father's Wish,* Christine Flynn's story of
a man searching for his lost love and child. Reader favorite
Marie Ferrarella is also back with a poignant story in
Brooding Angel. And a mother's determination not only
reunites her with her child but finds her a ready-made family
in Arlene James's *Child of Her Heart.*

In Trisha Alexander's latest, *The Girl Next Door* decides her
best friend, a freewheeling bachelor and sexy confidant, is the
man she's been looking for all her life. Now she just has to
convince him that they're falling in love. And we wrap up the
month of June by welcoming a new author to **Special Edition**.
A Family for Ronnie by Julie Caille is a touching story sure to
warm your hearts.

So don't miss a moment of these wonderful books. It's just
the beginning of a summer filled with love and romance from
Special Edition!

Sincerely,

Tara Gavin
Senior Editor

Please address questions and book requests to:
Silhouette Reader Service
U.S.: 3010 Walden Ave., P.O. Box 1325, Buffalo, NY 14269
Canadian: P.O. Box 609, Fort Erie, Ont. L2A 5X3

TRISHA ALEXANDER

THE GIRL NEXT DOOR

Silhouette®

SPECIAL EDITION®

Published by Silhouette Books

America's Publisher of Contemporary Romance

This book is dedicated to all the wonderful readers who have taken the
time to write to me over the past few years. You have amused me with
your comments and suggestions, inspired me with your encouragement and
praise, amazed me with your support and loyalty, and touched me with
your confidences and friendship. Thank you from the bottom of my heart.

Special thanks to Anita Molina for planting the idea of a book about best
friends and to fellow author Jan Freed for sharing her expertise concerning
the advertising business.

 SILHOUETTE BOOKS

ISBN 0-373-09965-7

THE GIRL NEXT DOOR

Copyright © 1995 by Patricia A. Kay

Books by Trisha Alexander

Silhouette Special Edition

Cinderella Girl #640
When Somebody Loves You #748
When Somebody Needs You #784
Mother of the Groom #801
When Somebody Wants You #822
Here Comes the Groom #845
Say You Love Me #875
What Will the Children Think? #906
Let's Make It Legal #924
The Real Elizabeth Hollister... #940
The Girl Next Door #965

TRISHA ALEXANDER

has had a lifelong love affair with books and always wanted to be a writer. She also loves cats, movies, the ocean, music, Broadway shows, cooking, traveling, being with her family and friends, Cajun food, *Calvin and Hobbes* and getting mail. Trisha and her husband have three grown children, two adorable grandchildren, and live in Houston, Texas. Trisha loves to hear from readers. You can write to her at P.O. Box 441603, Houston, TX 77244-1603.

Chapter One

Jenny Randall sat back on her heels and surveyed her front flower beds with satisfaction. For the past hour and a half, she'd been doing spring planting, and the results were gratifying.

A riot of colors teased the eye: bright red impatiens, pink begonias, yellow pansies, deep purple verbena, and white jasmine.

Tomorrow she would work on the small garden out back, she decided. She planned to plant cherry tomatoes and green onions, and maybe some herbs.

Jenny loved gardening, a fact which was a continuing source of surprise to her mother, Lois, because when Jenny was growing up she'd never shown the slightest interest in it.

About six years ago, though, she had interviewed a wealthy eighty-something Houstonian famous for her magnificent gardens, and that had triggered her interest. Then, when her great-aunt Jenny had died, leaving her this house, she had become totally hooked.

Jenny stretched contentedly. Her muscles ached, but it was a good kind of ache. Different from the muscle stiffness she experienced on the job. Some days, when she'd been sitting for hours—editing copy at her desk or typing up a story—she longed to be outdoors doing something physical. Today had been one of those days. But she felt fine now, and look what she'd accomplished.

She began loading her gardening tools into the bucket she used as a carryall. Just as she finished, she heard the sound of a car pulling into her narrow gravel driveway.

She stood, looked around, then smiled and waved.

Simon Christopher, her best friend for the past ten years, grinned back. He opened the door of his red Corvette convertible, climbed out and walked toward her, carrying a white plastic bag in his right hand. "Hey, the flowers look great!" he said enthusiastically.

Simon's unflagging optimism and good spirits were two of the qualities that had attracted Jenny to him so long ago, although sometimes relentless good cheer could get on a person's nerves....

Hurriedly, she dismissed the disloyal thought. "Thanks," she said, giving him a bigger smile because she felt guilty about what she'd been thinking.

"Are you going to help me plan my flower beds when the house is finished?"

Simon had torn down the sixty-three-year-old house he'd bought several years ago and was having a new, very contemporary home built in its place. In the meantime, he'd rented the house next door so that he could keep a close eye on the construction.

"Shoot, Simon, you can afford to hire someone professional to do that."

"I'd rather have you."

"Sure. Why not? Cheap labor."

His dark blue eyes, which always reminded Jenny of the ocean, twinkled. "I brought some Chinese." He held the bag up.

The aroma of General Tso's Chicken drifted her way, and Jenny's stomach growled in answer. Yet even though she was hungry, and his gesture was thoughtful, she felt like strangling him.

"Simon! Why didn't you call and *ask* me if I wanted to eat Chinese tonight?"

His face fell. "But you love Chinese . . ."

She sighed. "I know, but I happen to have a meal in the Crockpot."

He grimaced. "Oh."

She sighed again. "Yes. Oh."

There was silence between them for a few moments. Then he grinned again, his dimples cutting deep grooves in his face. "Tell you what. Put your dinner in the freezer. I'll come over and help you eat it some other night. And tonight we'll eat Chinese." He looked immensely pleased with himself, reminding her of the way Calvin and Hobbes, her two male cats, strutted around after catching an unsuspecting sparrow in the backyard.

Jenny bit back the sarcastic reply that was on the tip of her tongue. What was the use? Simon was Simon. If he made assumptions about her and about their friendship, it was her own fault. All these years, she'd allowed him to take her for granted. If she wanted his behavior to change, she was going to have to start doing things differently.

"I got all your favorites," he continued happily. "General Tso's Chicken, Happy Family, spring rolls and shrimp toast."

"I thought you had a date tonight."

"Yeah, well, I did." His expression turned sheepish. "Let's go inside. I'll tell you about it while we eat."

Simon headed for the kitchen while Jenny detoured into the one bathroom her little house contained. As she washed her hands and splashed water on her face, then quickly ran a brush through her short hair and applied fresh lipstick, she tried to rid herself of the negative feelings Simon had brought about by his actions.

In fairness, he didn't deserve her anger. He had always treated her this way, always assumed she would be ready, willing and available and would cheerfully fall into his plans, whatever they were. He hadn't changed at all in the ten years she'd known him.

But she had.

She sighed. Yes. That was exactly the problem. She had changed, and Simon hadn't noticed.

That's not his fault. Now, get out there and enjoy the evening. You can think about all of this later.

By the time she joined him in the tiny kitchen, she had regained her equilibrium. She saw that Simon had already set the round table with plates, napkins and utensils and had opened the cartons of food. He'd even poured her a glass of water.

Again, a flash of irritation shot through Jenny. Maybe she didn't want water. Maybe she wanted iced tea or milk. Couldn't he at least ask? He acted as if she was completely predictable. *Well, face it. For ten years, you have been.*

She walked over to the counter and turned off her slow cooker. Then she sat down and told herself she'd better chill out or else Simon would wonder what was wrong with her. Picking up her water glass, she took a swallow. "So what happened with your date?"

"I canceled out." He handed her the spring rolls.

"Why?"

He shrugged. "I don't know. I just wasn't excited about going." He heaped rice on his plate, then helped himself to a generous portion of the chicken.

Jenny took a spring roll and dipped it into hot mustard sauce. She took a bite. "Something happen that I don't know about?"

He shook his head. "Nothing happened. I'm just not going to be dating Melinda anymore."

Jenny nodded sagely. "Oh, I get it. Another Barbie doll bites the dust." Jenny referred to all Simon's women friends as Barbie dolls because they were all alike. Tall and slim. Blond and blue-eyed. Long-legged and beautiful. And they all had big breasts.

Jenny hated them all, probably because she was short and tiny, had dark hair and eyes and decidedly *small* breasts. She was not beautiful by anyone's stretch of the imagination.

People always called her "cute," a term she despised. Just once in her life, she wanted someone to refer to her as beautiful or sexy or glamorous or anything other than the "C" word.

"I'm sick of the dating scene. I think I'm gonna give it up completely," Simon said.

"That'll be the day."

He stopped in the middle of taking a bite. "What? You don't think I mean it?"

"Nope."

"What makes you say that?"

Jenny continued to shake her head. "Oh, you're just tired of Melinda, the way you eventually get tired of all of them. But you'll find another. You always do." Jenny tried to keep the bitterness she felt out of her voice. It would never do for Simon to think she was jealous.

"Maybe that has been true, in the past, but things are changing. I'm changing."

"Umm," was all Jenny said. So far, she'd seen no indication that Simon had changed at all. She took a helping of the Happy Family and continued eating.

"Oh, listen, I almost forgot," he said. "Nobody's using the Rockets tickets tomorrow night, so we can go to the game."

All of Jenny's irritation and frustration returned with the force of a small tornado. "I don't think so," she said tightly.

"Why not? You *love* the Rockets games."

"Yes, I know I do." *Drop it, Simon. Just drop it.*

"Then why don't you want to go?"

Jenny carefully laid down her fork. She took a deep breath before meeting his gaze. Her words were measured and even as she spoke. "Simon, did it ever occur to you that I might have other plans for tomorrow night?"

He stared at her. "Oh. Uh, do you?"

"After all, tomorrow *is* Friday," she said as if he hadn't spoken at all. "Maybe I have a date."

"A date!"

"Yes, Simon, you know. A date. That thing you're supposedly not going to do anymore. Where a man and woman go out together for a social evening, which might or might not lead to romance."

"Who do you have a date with?" he said disbelievingly.

She shrugged. "No one you know."

After a minute, a slow smile spread over his face. "Aw, come on, Jenny. You're pulling my leg. You don't have a date."

Jenny felt like kicking him. "You know, Simon, sometimes you can be really exasperating." She wiped her mouth with her napkin and threw it down on her plate. He was more than exasperating. He was also blind.

And stupid. Don't forget stupid!

His smile faded, to be replaced by a perplexed frown. "Did I say something wrong? Jenny, what's the matter?" He reached across the table to touch her hand. "Are you mad at me, or something?"

Her heart started to beat faster, and she swallowed hard. *Be cool. Be careful.* She took a deep breath and gently pulled her hand away. "No, Simon, I'm not mad at you, or *something,* but did you ever stop to think that maybe even friends might not appreciate being taken for granted?" She met his gaze evenly. "And is it so inconceivable that I *might* have a date?"

"No, of course not. You know I didn't mean that."

"Oh, I think you meant exactly that." And his inference hurt. It hurt a lot.

"No! Jenny, why would you think...hell..." He stopped in confusion. "It's just that we tell each other everything, and you haven't mentioned any guy lately."

No, I haven't mentioned any guy lately. In fact, I haven't mentioned any other man besides you for years. You're right about that. But you're dead wrong about something else, Simon. I do not tell you everything.

"So who is he? Someone from work? What's his name?" Simon said.

"I prefer not to discuss the subject right now," Jenny answered stiffly. "In fact, I'm really tired. I've had a long day, and I've got a headache." God, how many lies did that make? Three? Four? She stood.

Simon's face was a picture of bewilderment. If Jenny hadn't been so angry, with him and herself, she might have laughed. He looked as if he wanted to say something. He even opened his mouth, then shut it again. Eyeing her warily, he picked up his plate and carried it to the sink. Jenny started to tell him he didn't have to stay and help clean up, then thought better of it.

They had always shared the work equally, no matter what they were doing. That was another quality of Simon's she'd always appreciated—his willingness to do dishes or cook or anything else that might need doing. He had always treated her fairly, had never expected her to wait on him because she was a woman and he was a man.

Within minutes, they'd disposed of all remnants of their meal, and the kitchen was once again spotless, just the way Jenny liked it.

"Well, I guess I'll be going," he said. He ran his hand through his dark hair, messing up its perfect razor cut.

The action told her he was ill at ease. She wished she could say something to dispel the tension, but maybe it was best that he just go. Considering the mood she was in, if he stuck around much longer, she might say something she shouldn't. "I'll walk you outside," she said.

He headed out of the kitchen and down the hall, Jenny following. She'd always loved watching Simon walk. He had the nice, easy stride of an athlete and the long legs and broad shoulders to go with it. Tonight, dressed in loose-fitting cotton pants and a dark T-shirt, he looked particularly virile and attractive.

He opened the screen door and stood aside, allowing her to precede him outdoors. The air was scented with the sweet smell of freshly mown grass, and Jenny took a deep breath. The balmy spring evening was filled with the sounds of their West University neighborhood: the next-door neighbor's stereo playing hot jazz, muted voices in conversation somewhere down the street, cicadas singing in the trees with a lone mockingbird providing backup, a couple of dogs barking and the buzz of a ten-speed flying by.

Jenny looked up. The navy night was studded with stars, and a huge round moon smiled down at them. It was a perfect night for lovers. The thought caused a lonely ache to surround her heart.

"Jenny..."

Jenny reluctantly looked at Simon.

"Do you want to have lunch together tomorrow? I'll take you to Pappadeaux," he said, naming her favorite Cajun seafood restaurant.

"I can't. I'm going to Becky's." Becky was one of her older sisters. Jenny wasn't sure if she was glad she had a reason to refuse or disappointed that she couldn't go. She knew his invitation was his way of apologizing for whatever it was that had disturbed her tonight.

"Oh, okay. Guess I'll see you in the morning, then." Simon was referring to their normal routine of a morning run at a nearby track. He hesitated a moment, then bent down and brushed her cheek lightly with his lips.

Something sharp and painful spiraled through her at his casual caress. Suddenly, Jenny's eyes filled with tears, and she hurriedly turned away, saying, "'Night. Thanks for dinner."

She barely made it into the house before the tears burst forth. Angry with herself, she knuckled them away and fought to get herself under control. God, she was so stupid!

She laughed mirthlessly, remembering Simon's words from earlier in the evening. *We tell each other everything.* Ha! Like *hell* they did!

Maybe Simon told Jenny everything. But Jenny had been keeping something from Simon.

Something important.

In fact, her secret was the most important part of her life.

He would be shocked if he knew it.

For Jenny was deeply, irrevocably and hopelessly in love with Simon Christopher and had been for a long time.

Simon stood at the window of his twentieth-floor Galleria-area office and gazed out at the bustling city below. In the distance was Houston's impressive downtown skyline—just visible in the morning mist, which hadn't yet burned off.

He always felt a sense of pride when he saw the skyline. He really loved Houston, which surprised him. Most people who grew up in the hill country, as he had, thought of Houston as too big, too dirty and too crime ridden. Yet, Houston's energy and we-can-do-anything attitude had turned out to be exactly what he was looking for.

He'd been here eight years now, ever since he'd graduated from the University of Texas in Austin. And every day he discovered new facets of his adopted city.

And if it hadn't been for Jenny, he probably would never have come to Houston. He frowned slightly, thinking of Jenny. She hadn't come to the track this morning. It wasn't like her to miss their morning run.

Ever since he'd left her house last night, he'd been wondering if he'd said or done something wrong. Had he hurt her feelings with his doubts about her having a date? Hell, he hoped not. He wouldn't hurt Jenny's feelings for the world. He loved her like a sister. More, even. He and his sister, Samantha, had never been as close as he and Jenny were.

His frown faded as he remembered the day he'd met her. He'd walked into the office of the *Daily Texan*, the UT student newspaper, and the first person he'd laid eyes on had been this little dark-haired, dark-eyed dynamo with an infectious laugh and more enthusiasm and idealism and determination than he'd ever encountered in one person.

They'd become almost instant friends—sharing a closeness that defied description. They could talk about anything and did. They both had quick minds and a wealth of interests. They both loved sports and movies and books. They could discuss a book or a movie or a game for hours, debating the pros and cons.

Their friendship had weathered a lot of ups and downs, too: the death of Simon's brother, Stephen, five years ago in a freak climbing accident; the traumatic end of Jenny's relationship with that jerk Travis what's-his-name, who was never good enough for her, anyway; the death of Jenny's great-aunt after a lingering illness during which Jenny had lived with her and nursed her; and the meteoric success of Simon's advertising agency.

The buzz of Simon's intercom broke into his thoughts. He walked over to his desk and pressed a button. "Yes?"

Cherry, the firm's receptionist and switchboard operator, said, "Jenny Randall's on line two."

Simon grinned and picked up the receiver. "Great minds... I was just thinking about you."

"Were you?"

"Yeah, just remembering how you persuaded me to move to Houston, which turned out to be the best decision I ever made." He sat on the edge of his desk and played with the Waterford paperweight Jenny had given him for his thirtieth birthday—the one with the Astros logo engraved in it. It one was of his most prized possessions.

"If I'd known you were going to become some kind of supersalesman, I'm not sure I would have tried so hard," she said.

He chuckled. "You never give up, do you?" He enjoyed their ongoing disagreement about his choice of career because Jenny was so doggedly determined never to admit that what he did for a living just might have a redeeming quality or two.

"Never. Listen, Simon, the reason I called is…I'm sorry about last night. I had some things on my mind, and I took my worries out on you."

Relief washed over him. "Hey, no problem. Anything you want to talk about?"

"No," she said softly, "but thanks."

"I'm always ready to listen."

"I know that."

"Jen?"

"Yes?"

He hesitated. "It—it's not financial problems, is it?" he said hurriedly, "because if it is, you know the offer of a job is always open."

She laughed. "I know, but I'm not *that* desperate!"

He laughed, too. "One of these days, I'm gonna convince you to come to work for me."

"In your dreams…"

"You change your mind about tonight's game?" The minute the words were out of his mouth, he could have kicked himself. Jeez, that sounded as if he hadn't believed her story that she had other plans. He held his breath. Was she going to lambaste him again?

"No, I still can't go."

He let out the breath. She wasn't mad. "What about tomorrow morning? You planning to run?"

"I don't know. Depends."

They talked a few more minutes, then hung up. Simon continued to sit on the edge of his desk while he rehashed the phone call. He wished she'd tell him what was bothering her. He'd like the chance to help. After all, what were friends for?

And who was she going out with tonight? And why wouldn't she tell him about it? Was it someone she thought he'd disapprove of? Another jerk like Travis who would take advantage of her generosity and warm heart and walk all over her? Even the thought made Simon's blood boil.

He put down the paperweight and stood.

Just then, there was a sharp triple-knock on his door.

"Come on in," he called, knowing by the knock that it was his partner, Mark Alonzo.

Sure enough, Mark, nattily dressed in a dark blue pin-striped suit, black hair slicked back, dark eyes bright and shrewd, strode in.

Simon grinned at him. He and Mark were opposites in many ways, but they made a hell of a team— Simon providing the bulk of the creative ideas and Mark providing the business acumen.

"Hey, buddy," Mark said, "you mind if I take off early today? Brooke and I want to fly down to Padre for the weekend."

"Of course I don't mind." Through the first four days of the week, Mark normally put in ten-to-twelve-hour days, but he and his wife enjoyed getting away early on Fridays.

Mark sat on one of the gray suede chairs flanking Simon's desk, and Simon sat in his desk chair. "You want to come with us?"

"Three's a crowd," Simon said, although the offer was tempting. Simon loved the beach, and he especially loved Padre Island. Brooke's parents owned a beach house in one of the few secluded areas left, and Simon thought longingly of the peaceful spot.

"We don't mind."

Simon shook his head. "Thanks, I appreciate the offer, but I don't think so."

"Okay. We should be back Sunday night, as long as the weather holds out."

"Don't worry about it. I'll hold the fort."

Mark and Brooke were flying freaks. They owned a small twin-engine Beechcraft and took it up every chance they got. That's how they'd met—taking flying lessons at the same time.

After Mark left, Simon sighed again. It would have been nice to be able to join Mark and Brooke. But he had no intention of horning in on their weekend.

Simon swiveled around and stared out the window again. Mark's invitation had pointed out a recurring problem. With the exception of Jenny, all Simon's friends were married.

It used to be that if he wanted to go skiing in Colorado or scuba diving in the Caribbean, all he had to do was pick up the phone and any one of half a dozen guys would be ready, willing and eager to go with him.

Nowadays, all those same guys were half of a couple, and they took their spur-of-the-moment weekend trips with the other half.

The way Mark and Brooke were doing this weekend.

Simon wished he had someone to take spur-of-the-moment trips with. He knew he could easily find a willing woman to accompany him, but in this respect, he was old-fashioned. He believed that traveling with a woman signified a certain type of relationship.

The kind of relationship that led to marriage.

And so far, Simon had not met any woman he wanted to marry.

As a matter of fact, he hadn't met any woman he could even *imagine* marrying.

He thought of the women he'd dated the past few years. He tried to picture spending the rest of his life with any of them. He couldn't. What in the world would they talk about?

Yet, despite the fact that he had no one suitable in mind, his thoughts had been turning more and more toward marriage. He'd meant it last night when he'd told Jenny that he was sick of the dating scene.

For a while now, he'd been wanting something different. After all, he was thirty years old. It was time for him to settle down, maybe have a family. His parents certainly thought so. They'd been gently nudging him in that direction for at least two years.

But Jenny was right. Barbie dolls were good to look at, but if he was going to spend the rest of his life with someone, he wanted someone who had something upstairs.

He wondered if Jenny ever thought about getting married. Funny... but they'd never discussed the subject. Surely she must think about it. Didn't every woman want to get married? And Jenny was crazy about kids. He thought about how good she was with her sisters' kids and smiled. Yeah, Jenny would make a great mother.

He made a mental note to talk to her about the subject of marriage, see if she'd been having the same kinds of feelings he'd been having. And even if she wasn't thinking along those lines, herself, she was bound to have some ideas about how he might go about accomplishing his goal. Yeah, Jenny had a good head on her shoulders. She could probably give him some sensible advice. Tell him what he was doing wrong.

That was a great idea!

And it would kill two birds.

Because if he got Jenny to thinking about his dilemma, she'd soon forget about her own troubles.

With a self-satisfied smile, he turned his chair around and settled in to do a day's work.

Chapter Two

"Jenny, you haven't forgotten about career day at Kendall's school, have you?"

Jenny and her sister were eating lunch outside on Becky's patio, enjoying the mild March weather before the onset of Houston's suffocatingly hot summer.

"No, I haven't forgotten. And Simon suggested that you ask Brooke Alonzo."

"Really?" Becky said eagerly. "Gee, that'd be great. Kendall will be thrilled." Brooke Alonzo was a local TV anchorwoman. "But would she be willing to talk to a bunch of fourth-graders?"

"Simon said she'd be glad to do it. Do you want me to ask her for you?"

"Would you?"

"Sure. Simon offered to come talk to the kids, too, but I wasn't sure they'd be very interested in the advertising business." She laughed. "He, of course, is sure they'd hang on his every word." Jenny expected Becky to laugh and agree with her.

Instead, she gave her a thoughtful look and said, "Jenny, do you realize how often you mention Simon's name in conversation?"

Jenny eyed her sister over her glass of lemonade. She hoped her expression didn't reveal how Becky's unexpected comment had unnerved her. Setting the glass down, she shrugged casually. "Well, that's only natural, don't you think? After all, he's my best friend. Heck, you're always quoting Rhonda." Rhonda was Becky's best friend.

Jenny took a bite of her tuna fish sandwich and hoped she hadn't protested too much. Slowly, she met her sister's gaze.

Becky's dark brown eyes, identical in color to Jenny's, looked entirely too perceptive. "So you and Simon are still just friends, huh?"

Jenny didn't like Becky's tone. She *must* be suspicious. "Do you have a problem with that?"

"Nooo . . . I guess not."

"Then why did you ask?"

Now Becky shrugged. "I don't know. I was . . . just wondering."

"You must have had a reason for wondering." Was she that transparent? Were people beginning to suspect what Jenny's true feelings were? The thought gave Jenny a sinking feeling.

She had never confided her feelings for Simon to anyone, not even Becky, and she was closer to Becky than to anyone else in her family. Oh, brother. That would be all she needed! It was bad enough to be hopelessly in love with a man who thought of her as a pal. Having her family know about her unrequited feelings and having them pity her would be unendurable.

Becky traced a pattern in the condensation on her glass. "I guess I find it odd that the two of you spend so much time together, yet are only friends," she said slowly.

"Why is it odd?"

"You know…a man and woman…" Becky's voice trailed off.

"Don't you think men and women can be friends? Does there always have to be some kind of romantic relationship between them?"

"No, I guess not. But—"

"But what?"

"Oh, I don't know." Becky shrugged again. "Don't pay any attention to me." She smiled brightly. "How *is* Simon, by the way? We haven't seen much of him the past few months."

"He's fine. Really busy with the agency and the new house." Jenny wasn't about to confess to her sister that she had purposely stopped inviting Simon to family activities because she was afraid her family, knowing her as well as they did, would inevitably figure out exactly how she felt about him.

"He's really made a success of the agency, hasn't he?" Becky said, an admiring note in her voice.

Jenny nodded and thought how any one of her sisters would be more suited to Simon than she was. They all equated success in terms of how much money a man made, whereas Jenny wasn't at all impressed by Simon's money. In fact, she thought he'd sold out.

"He must be making pots of money if he can afford to tear down his house and put up a brand-new one in its place."

"I guess he is. We don't discuss money." Again not strictly the truth. Only this morning Simon had asked her if she was having financial problems, and he was always making cracks about the pittance Jenny was paid in her capacity as editor of the *Village Vanguard,* the weekly newspaper that served West U, where they both lived. He constantly tried to talk her into coming to work for him, but Jenny would never do that. She hadn't gotten a journalism degree to spend her time writing advertising copy to persuade people to buy stuff they didn't need.

Besides the fact that it was torture enough to spend so much of her free time with Simon. If she saw him every day, all day long, was forced to witness him flirting with other women as she was sure he did, she would be utterly miserable.

"Money's all Jimmy and I *ever* discuss," Becky said.

Jenny looked up. It was on the tip of her tongue to remind Becky that Jimmy was her husband and Simon was just Jenny's friend, but the expression on her sister's face stopped her and for the first time since the subject of Simon had been introduced, Jenny forgot her own problems. "Beck... are you and Jimmy having money problems?"

"No more than usual."

Jenny knew it must be hard raising three kids on one salary. And Jimmy couldn't make all that much managing a grocery store.

"He keeps harping about me getting a job," Becky said. "And I keep telling him that until the kids are in school, it doesn't make sense. I mean, I'd pay just about everything I could earn in child care. It's not like he has regular hours, either, so I couldn't depend on him for much in the way of help."

Jenny nodded. Her sister was right.

Becky sighed. "You know, Jen, sometimes I'm really envious of you... having only yourself to worry about." She grimaced. "And no one to answer to." She looked up, her gaze meeting Jenny's. "Sometimes I dream about running away from home."

"You don't really mean that," Jenny said. "You're just frustrated right now."

"I guess..." But Becky didn't sound convinced.

"Look, anytime you get to thinking I have some kind of ideal life, I want you to remember something."

"What?"

"Despite a shortage of money, you are a very fortunate woman. You're married to a good man who loves you, and you have three beautiful and highly intelligent children."

Becky's eyes twinkled. "This is true." She chuckled. "You left out perfectly behaved..."

Jenny grinned. "That, too."

Becky's smile slowly faded, and she pleated her napkin. "I know you're right. It's just that sometimes... oh, I don't know... I just get tired of never having any money... of always worrying about something...like Kendall needing braces and Kelly wanting to take gymnastics.'' Becky sighed. ''It costs so much to raise kids nowadays.''

''Even so, I'd trade places with you in a heartbeat. There's nothing I want more than to get married and have a family.''

''Aw, Jen...'' Becky abandoned the napkin and reached across the table to touch Jenny's hand.

Jenny snatched it away. ''I didn't say that to make you feel sorry for me. I just wanted to give you another perspective.''

Becky nodded. ''I know.'' Her smile was sheepish. ''Thanks, Jen. I guess sometimes I *do* need reminding of how lucky I am.''

''We all do at times.'' Jenny guessed she was no exception. ''Remember, the grass always looks greener in someone else's yard.'' She wiped her mouth with her napkin and stood. ''I've gotta run. You know how busy Fridays are. Thanks for lunch.''

''I guess I'll see you at Mom and Dad's this weekend?'' Becky stood, too.

''Yeah. I'll be there for Sunday dinner, as usual.''

The sisters hugged, exchanged ''love you's'' and Jenny left.

Ten minutes later, driving back to her office, she thought about her conversation with Becky. What she'd said about trading places with her sister was true.

Although Jenny loved her job and knew she would always want to work in her field—in fact, her dream was to eventually write a syndicated editorial column similar to those of Anna Quindlen and Linda Ellerbee—she had never seen herself as a career woman.

She came from a warm, loving family, and she wanted a warm, loving family of her own.

As long as you keep mooning over a man who considers you a friend and nothing more, that's not likely to happen, she reminded herself as she pulled into the small parking lot behind the building housing the newspaper.

She sighed. Maybe it was time to make some changes in her life. Maybe she should try to forget about Simon. Put him out of her life completely.

As Jenny walked into the building, she smiled wryly. The only way she would be able to forget about Simon was to move away. As far away from Houston as she could get.

The thought gave her the emptiest feeling.

Never to see Simon.

Never to hear his low, sexy laugh.

Never to watch his expressive face or to see those deep dimples when he smiled. Never to gaze into those riveting blue eyes. Oh, God, how could she bear it? Yet how could she endure the status quo?

It was getting harder and harder to be in Simon's company and keep up a facade. Look at last night. She'd nearly lost it. She knew that one of these days she was bound to give herself away.

And then what?

Things would never be the same between her and Simon if he suspected that her feelings for him had gone beyond friendship. He would feel uncomfortable with her, things would become awkward and their friendship would slowly be destroyed.

She would lose him completely.

Now she felt sick.

Face it, Jenny, you're in a no-win situation.

Entering her office, she glumly tossed her briefcase onto her cluttered desk and plopped into her swivel chair.

"Hey, Randall! You look like you just lost your best friend. Something wrong?"

Jenny looked up. Pete Cramer, the production manager and a really nice guy, stood in her open doorway. She shook off her unhappy thoughts and smiled at him. "No, nothing's wrong, just preoccupied, I guess."

"You sure?"

"I'm sure."

For the rest of the afternoon, as she edited copy and answered phone calls and did all the last-minute things that needed doing before the weekly deadline, her thoughts kept returning to her problem.

She knew she had to take some kind of action soon. Because if even her co-workers were beginning to think something was wrong with her, things had reached a point where she could no longer continue as she had been.

Jenny had intended to skip her morning run—she wasn't sure she could handle seeing Simon yet—but the following day, she found herself driving to the track at six-thirty in the morning the way she always did.

As she pulled into the school parking lot, she saw Simon's Corvette parked near the gate, and her heart gave a tiny hop in anticipation of seeing him.

She climbed out of her eight-year-old Ford and walked toward the track. Morning mist silvered the grass in the large oval center of the track, and a pinky lavender tinted the eastern sky.

Through the muted morning light, she saw Simon walking toward her. Usually, she could control her emotions better, but this morning—maybe because she'd been thinking about him so much for the past twenty-four hours and was feeling so vulnerable—the sight of him caused something to tighten in her chest. *I shouldn't have come today.*

He grinned as he got closer.

"Hey," he said cheerfully, "you missed a great game last night."

"I saw where they won big-time."

He nodded as they began to do their stretching exercises. "Wouldn't surprise me to see them go all the way this year."

Jenny nodded. "So, did you find someone to go to the game with you?"

"I didn't even try. Just went by myself."

"What about Mark and Brooke? Didn't they go, too?"

"Nope. They went down to Padre yesterday afternoon."

Jenny nodded.

"So how was your date?"

Oh, why had she continued to let him believe she'd had a date? She hated lying. She hated any kind of subterfuge. "Fine."

"Just fine? Where did you go?"

"We didn't go anywhere." She forestalled another question by adding, "Look, can we drop the subject? I'm not in the mood to discuss this."

He gave her a sidelong look. "Okay."

For the next few minutes, they didn't talk. She wondered if she'd hurt his feelings. Well, if she had, that was his problem. He shouldn't be so nosy.

Once they'd finished stretching, they moved onto the track. About a half mile into their run, Simon said, "You know, yesterday after you called, I started wondering about something."

"What?"

"Do you ever think about getting married?"

Jenny's heart gave an alarming lurch, and she nearly stumbled.

Simon's arm shot out to steady her. "Hey, you okay?"

"Yeah, I'm fine. Stupid rock." There hadn't been any rock in her path, but she certainly didn't want him to know how much his question had thrown her.

"So, do you . . . think about getting married?" he said once their pace evened out again.

"Occasionally. Why?" Jenny waved to a fellow runner—an older man who ran every morning about the same time she and Simon did.

"I've been thinking about it a lot lately."

If she hadn't known that he wasn't seeing anyone, Jenny was sure she might have given her feelings away, because even the thought of Simon marrying someone else made her ache inside. "Have you?" She was proud of the casual way she asked the question.

"Yeah." He gave her a sidelong glance. "I've got a problem, though."

I know the feeling.

"As much as I hate to admit it, you're right about the women I've dated the past few years. They really *are* . . . well . . . kind of empty-headed."

"Why do you hate to admit it?" She angled her gaze his way and grinned. She was determined to act as if this conversation was perfectly normal.

"No man likes to admit he's been stupid."

"No man likes to admit he's been *wrong* . . . about anything."

He chuckled. "Look who's talking. The original stubborn mule."

"Who, *moi?*" Jenny had been called stubborn all of her life. When she was little, her mother used to say she had a stubborn streak a mile wide. Her father always laughed and said she was the most hardheaded kid he'd ever met.

"Well, anyway, you were right this time, I'm afraid."

"So what's your point?"

"My point is, I don't want to marry one of those women. I want to marry someone I can talk to. And so far, I haven't met anyone like that."

The ache in her chest, the one she was trying to ignore, expanded until it was one great, agonizing pain. *Are you blind?* she wanted to cry. *Am I invisible?* She concentrated on breathing in and out, concentrated on not showing any emotion, concentrated on squashing down the hurt. The sound of their pounding footsteps filled her brain and echoed her throbbing misery.

"So what do you think?" Simon said.

"About what?"

"Come on, Jenny. . . what am I doing wrong?"

Suddenly Jenny realized she'd had enough. It was bad enough to feel the way she did. But this . . . this discussion, this call for advice, was beyond what anyone should have to endure. There was no way she was going to counsel Simon on his love life or help him find someone else to marry so her heart could be broken.

"Look, Simon, I'm not Ann Landers. Anyway, now that you're going to start thinking with your upper anatomy instead of your lower, you should have no trouble solving your own problems."

Jenny tried to forget about her conversation with Simon for the remainder of the weekend, but it wasn't easy. She was grateful she had so much to do.

By Monday morning, she was back on track again. Monday was production day at the paper. The atmosphere was fraught with emergencies on the verge of happening. Everyone from the clerks at the front counter to the proofreader back in her cubbyhole worked at top speed. Hardly anyone even took a lunch hour, and a lot of junk food was consumed.

As the editor, Jenny tried to have all the last-minute editorial copy to the typesetter before noon, which meant she was usually swamped the entire morning.

At ten o'clock, her intercom buzzed. It was Gloria Holmberg, the publisher and Jenny's boss. "Jenny?" she said. "Could you come into my office, please?"

"Sure. Be right there." Jenny laid down her red pencil, tucked her blouse more securely into the waistband of her slacks and put on her jacket. Thirty seconds later, she tapped on Gloria's closed door.

"Come on in."

Jenny opened the door and entered the large, sun-filled room. Although the decor and furnishings of the rest of the offices were utilitarian and bland, Gloria's office reflected her personality. Plush seafoam carpeting complemented gleaming mahogany furniture. Dozens of lush well-tended plants graced the room, and Gloria's collection of crystal paperweights sparkled brilliantly from their various vantage points.

Gloria looked up from her immaculate desk and smiled a welcome. She looked as elegantly turned out as her surroundings in her black-and-white linen dress, the perfect foil to her salt-and-pepper hair. A tiny woman whose delicate looks were deceptive and lulled unwary adversaries into thinking she would be an easy opponent, she was actually tough, smart and almost never lost a skirmish. "Shut the door behind you, will you?"

Jenny complied, then sat in one of the two jade chairs flanking Gloria's desk. It wasn't unusual to be called into her boss's office, so she wasn't concerned about the reason for this summons. Gloria believed in keeping lines of communication open and conferred with her department heads often.

Jenny admired her boss tremendously. Gloria's passion and vision, and the editorial focus she advocated, was the main reason Jenny had accepted the position at the *Vanguard* over better-paying offers.

Gloria looked at Jenny for a few moments before speaking. "Jenny, I've, uh, got something to tell you, and... well, it's hard to know where to begin." She sighed. "Oh, dear, this is more difficult than I thought it would be." She tapped her gold pen against the desktop.

A tiny frisson of alarm crept along Jenny's spine. Gloria was nervous! Something important must have happened. Until now, the only time Jenny had ever seen her boss rattled was the day Gloria's daughter gave birth to twins.

"Is something wrong?" she asked.

"No, nothing's wrong." Gloria sighed again, deeply. Then, looking Jenny straight in the eye, she said, "I've sold the paper."

The frisson exploded into gut-wrenching shock. Momentarily speechless, Jenny just stared at Gloria.

"I know you're surprised, and I'm sorry to spring it on you like this."

Surprised was an understatement. Flabbergasted, completely and utterly stunned—was more accurate. "I—I can't believe it," she finally managed to sputter.

"The deal has been in the works for weeks." Gloria sat back in her swivel chair, appearing more relaxed now. "I wanted to tell you about it, but I couldn't. So many things could have gone wrong, and I saw no reason to upset you or worry you needlessly."

"But I don't understand. I—I thought you *loved* the paper. You've told me, so many times, how the *Vanguard* is just like one of your children."

"I *do* love the paper, but things change." Gloria smiled sadly. "Circumstances change. It's getting more and more difficult for an independent weekly to survive in this day of big chains with big money behind them, you know that. And it's particularly difficult for a paper with our editorial policy."

Yes, Jenny did know that. She and Gloria and Megan Kimball, the advertising manager and Jenny's closest friend at the paper, had discussed this problem many times.

"But it's more than that," Gloria continued. "I'm tired. After twenty-three years in this business, I'm ready to retire. I have nothing left to prove. For a while now, I've been thinking about moving to Wimberley so I can be close to Shanna."

Shanna was Gloria's daughter—the one who had presented her with twin grandsons.

"I want to smell the roses, enjoy Paul and Patrick, get to see them grow up." Gloria's green eyes clouded. "I missed out on so much of Shanna's childhood. After Dave and I were divorced, and I spent such long hours here, whole days would go by when the only time I saw her was when she was sleeping."

Jenny nodded. She could understand those sentiments. Actually, she understood those sentiments much better than Gloria's admission that she was tired. But she couldn't help feeling somehow betrayed.

"Quite simply, I was offered a deal I couldn't refuse, at a time when I was ready to listen."

"Who bought the paper?"

"Evan Armstrong."

Evan Armstrong! Jenny swallowed. She had met Armstrong last fall at a newspaper convention in San Diego. He had been the keynote speaker. His company, Armstrong Communications, owned a chain of weeklies in California and, for the past few years, had been acquiring properties in other parts of the U.S.— mainly Florida, Arizona and Texas. Armstrong was a legend in the newspaper community. He had started forty years ago with one small paper and had expanded his holdings into a several-hundred-million-dollar corporation.

"He'll be here Wednesday to talk to the staff," Gloria said. "However, I plan to tell them about the sale this evening once we put the paper to bed." She leaned forward, her expression earnest and apologetic. "I wanted to tell you first because, of all the staff, your feelings about the paper are closest to mine and because I consider you more than an employee. You're a friend."

Tears stung Jenny's eyes. She fought against them. "I appreciate that," she said softly.

"Besides, in a sale like this, the editorial department is usually affected the most."

Jenny nodded. This she knew. She thought back to sales of other papers that were members of the same newspaper association the *Vanguard* belonged to. Some of those sales had meant drastic changes to the papers involved. "Has Mr. Armstrong indicated whether he plans to make any changes?"

"He's promised me that initially nothing will change. But I'm sure that eventually there will be changes. Each person puts his own mark on a property, you know that."

"Yes." Jenny's mind whirled. She still felt too stunned to assimilate what this sale would mean in terms of her future. "When do you plan to leave?"

Gloria shrugged. "I don't know yet. When Evan gets here Wednesday, we'll talk about it. I'll stay on as long as he wants me to. I want there to be a smooth transition."

Jenny nodded again. She bit her bottom lip and stared down at her hands. She couldn't think of anything else to say.

"Jenny..."

Jenny looked up.

"Maybe it's time for you to move on, too," Gloria said. "Your talents are really wasted here, and we both know it."

Easy enough for Gloria to say move on, Jenny thought with a trace of resentment. Jenny didn't have the advantage of money, the way Gloria did. Money gave a person the freedom to move and make changes. To take chances. To look for the kind of job that might lead to her realizing her dream of becoming a nationally syndicated columnist.

"I've got a lot of contacts in the business. I'd be happy to put in a word for you."

Jenny nodded.

"Well, I know I've given you a lot to think about," Gloria said.

Jenny knew a dismissal when she heard one. She stood.

Gloria smiled apologetically. "I know I don't have to remind you not to say anything about this to anyone else until my meeting with the staff this evening."

For the rest of the day, it was difficult for Jenny to concentrate on the immediate priority of the wrap-up of the week's work when everything Gloria had said, and all its ramifications, kept churning away in her mind.

Gloria's advice kept popping to the forefront of Jenny's thoughts. *Maybe it's time for you to move on, too.* Jenny thought about Simon, about her frustration and increasing unhappiness in that direction.

Maybe Gloria was right. Maybe it was time to at least attempt to change her life. Maybe the smartest thing she could do would be to look for a job somewhere else.

Somewhere far away from Houston . . . and Simon.

Chapter Three

Simon wasn't the type to brood.

Nevertheless, ever since Saturday morning when Jenny had been less than sympathetic when he'd wanted to discuss the problem of his finding someone to marry, he had been brooding.

What was her problem, anyway? He didn't appreciate that crack she'd made about him finally thinking with his upper anatomy instead of his lower.

Okay, maybe that *was* what he'd been doing, but did she have to say so in that sarcastic tone of voice?

Boy, she'd been in a damned funny mood the past couple of days. And he couldn't help feeling she'd taken out her unhappiness—if that's what it was—on him. He didn't feel he deserved that kind of treatment.

In fact, he thought she owed him an apology.

Knowing Jenny, he wouldn't get one, he thought ruefully. She was always so convinced her opinions were right. When he'd first met her, this absolute certainty of her convictions had been one of the qualities he had admired most. But lately, he had sometimes had the disloyal thought that Jenny was more than a little self-righteous.

Maybe the wisest thing he could do would be to give her a wide berth for a while. Maybe she just needed some time to work out her problems.

Simon decided that was a good idea, so he stayed away from her for the rest of the weekend. He didn't call her or drop by her house, and just as he'd thought, she didn't call him.

By Monday morning, though, he'd decided it was silly to keep avoiding her. He admitted to himself that he missed her.

Who cares who's at fault here? he asked himself. The point was, they'd been friends for too long to let something minor like this come between them.

He headed for the track determined to talk to her. He intended to find out what was bugging her, get it out in the open and help her deal with it.

She didn't show up.

Her absence bothered him more than anything she'd said or done up to that point. In the past few years, since they'd started running together, he could count on one hand the number of times Jenny had stayed away.

Yet just in the past week, she'd missed two mornings.

All Monday morning, he considered calling her, saying something like, "Now, dammit, this has gone on long enough. I think you owe it to me to tell me what's eating you!''

But something held him back. Maybe he held off calling because he knew how wild her Mondays usually were, and he hated adding to the stress of her day.

Or maybe he was just plain cowardly.

Around noon, Mark stuck his head in the door. ''Want to go to lunch?''

Simon had finally settled down to work on a new account, and he had been thinking he might skip lunch since he'd wasted so much time thinking about Jenny that morning. ''I don't know. What did you have in mind?''

Mark grinned. ''Rosie's?''

Rosie's was their favorite Mexican restaurant—a small, family-owned place tucked into a nondescript strip center on Bering Drive, about five minutes away from their office. Simon laid down his pen. ''You talked me into it.''

Fifteen minutes later, they sat across from each other in one of the leather booths overlooking the parking area, a big basket of warm tostadas and a dish of homemade salsa in front of them.

''You're sure quiet today,'' Mark said between mouthfuls.

''Yeah, I know.''

''Something wrong?''

''No, not really. I've just had something on my mind,'' Simon admitted. He dipped a chip and ate it.

''Anything you want to talk about?''

Simon met his partner's gaze. Although he and Mark were a winning combination at work and shared a comfortable friendship outside of the office, they had never confided much in each other about their personal lives.

Mark was sociable and agreeable, but he kept his private life private. And Simon pretty much felt the same way. Come to think of it, Jenny was his only confidante. The only confidante he'd ever had. Funny, he'd never realized that before.

He frowned. "Jenny's upset with me for some reason, and it's bugging the hell out of me. I have no idea what the problem is, and she won't tell me. She's just been real sarcastic and distant lately."

Mark finished chewing, then gave Simon a thoughtful look. "You two act more like an old married couple than old married couples do."

Simon, who had just taken a swallow of his iced tea, choked. "That's ridiculous," he finally managed to say.

"No, it's not."

"Mark, Jenny and I are *friends*. We don't have the kind of relationship you're talking about. We never have."

"Regardless, that's the way it strikes me."

For the rest of the day, Simon kept thinking about Mark's words. For some reason, he felt more disturbed than ever.

It was nine o'clock that night before the paper was finally ready for the printer. Earlier that evening, around seven, Gloria had sent out for barbecue. She had started the tradition of feeding the staff on Monday nights many years ago, and they all looked forward to it.

Everyone had been laughing and talking and eating and working. No one seemed to have the least premonition of the news in store for them later.

As soon as Pete finished checking the pages and pronounced the issue ready to go, Gloria said, "Before anyone leaves, I'd like to talk to all of you for a few moments, please."

Then she proceeded to tell them what she'd told Jenny earlier. Stunned gasps and shocked faces greeted her announcement, followed by stirrings and murmurings and a babble of questions.

Jenny watched the faces of the others—in particular, the department heads. She could see her own concern reflected in their eyes.

"I know your first concern is about your jobs and how secure they are," Gloria said, "which is only natural. In fact, that was one of my main concerns, too. But Mr. Armstrong has assured me that he foresees no personnel changes. In fact, he promised me that everyone will keep their job."

There was a collective sigh of relief.

Surreptitiously, Jenny and Pete exchanged a glance. His eyebrows quirked as if he, too, wondered just how long that promise would be kept.

"Nor does he intend to change the paper itself—at least not initially." Gloria gave them a reassuring smile. "He'll be here on Wednesday, and at that time he'll answer all of your questions."

Soon after, the meeting was over.

As the staff dispersed, Emma Goodman, the business manager cum bookkeeper, walked up to Jenny. Emma's blue eyes behind trifocals looked worried. She squeezed Jenny's forearm. "This is awful, Jenny," she said in a low voice.

Jenny tried to smile reassuringly. Emma had been with the paper for twenty-one of its twenty-three years. She was a kindly, sweet-natured sixty-three-year-old widow who was every employee's favorite shoulder to cry on and person to share happy news with.

Emma was everybody's mother, everybody's friend. Even if no one else remembered your birthday, she did, and inevitably brought in her famous Texas sheet cake to help you celebrate.

She was the first one to inquire after a sick child or to offer to baby-sit if you were in a bind.

When Jenny's great-aunt was dying, Emma had stopped by several times with chicken soup, flowers and lots of hugs.

At work she was loyal, dependable and discreet. There was no reason for her to stick around on Monday nights, but she always did.

"Maybe you'll need help," she always told Gloria. "I don't mind staying."

Jenny adored her.

And because she did, and didn't want Emma to worry, she pretended a nonchalance she didn't feel. But she wasn't sure Emma was buying it, because the older woman's eyes continued to look disturbed when she finally wandered off in the direction of her office, saying, "I'll see you Wednesday, Jenny."

"Bye, Emma."

By nine-thirty, everyone had gone home except for Jenny, Gloria and Pete. Jenny felt completely drained and gathered up her belongings. She was looking forward to a long soak in the tub tonight. And maybe a glass of her favorite Irish crème. She had a new Mary Higgins Clark novel she'd been looking forward to reading. Maybe she'd start it tonight.

Jenny didn't work on Tuesdays because she worked long days Fridays and Mondays. No one except the circulation department worked on Tuesdays. Thinking about her day off, she decided she might even skip her morning run again and just sleep in.

Why not? she thought. *I so seldom pamper myself, and with everything that's happened in the past few days here at the paper and between me and Simon, I think I deserve a little pampering.*

As Jenny walked down the hall toward the front door, she passed the open door to Gloria's office. "'Night, Gloria," she said.

Gloria looked up. "Would you like to have a drink with me before you go home?"

Jenny thought longingly of the hot bath, the Irish crème and the new book. The last thing she wanted to do was rehash the meeting and discuss the response of the staff to Gloria's announcement, but something in Gloria's eyes stopped her.

Instinctively, Jenny knew Gloria needed support right now. *So she's not as sure she's done the right thing as she wanted me to believe.* "Okay, but I can't stay long. I'm awfully tired."

They drove both their cars to a neighborhood bar a few blocks from the office. The two had gone there dozens of times before—particularly on Friday evenings after the last ad had been turned in and the paper had been dummied. It was a pleasant place frequented by regulars, quiet and perfect for talking.

Jenny ordered a glass of wine. Just one, she thought, then she would be firm about going home.

After they were served, Gloria met Jenny's gaze. "How do you think the announcement went over tonight?"

"As good as can be expected."

"I know everyone's upset, but it's going to be all right, really."

"I hope so."

"Armstrong told me one of the reasons he wanted the paper was the quality of the staff as well as the quality of the product."

Jenny knew that no matter what Armstrong had said, Gloria could not predict what he might eventually do. And she would certainly have no say-so if he *did* decide to make changes.

Gloria bit her bottom lip, a habit that revealed she was worried. "I did the only thing I could do, you know. In the end, this will be the best decision for everyone."

Jenny nodded noncommittally. It wasn't the only thing Gloria could have done, and they both knew it. And no matter how Gloria tried to justify the sale, Jenny would never believe it was the best decision for everyone.

"You're not angry with me, are you?"

Jenny sighed. "No, I'm not angry with you. I don't even blame you for selling. In your place, I would probably have done the same thing. But you can't expect me to be jumping up and down with joy. This is going to change a lot for me and for the others."

Gloria nodded.

They continued to talk as they finished their wine, but their conversation was strained. Jenny knew that Gloria needed to feel she'd done the right thing. She wanted Jenny's assurance that the staff would still like her and look up to her.

Jenny wanted to tell Gloria she couldn't have it both ways, then thought, what's the point? Why make Gloria feel worse than the woman already did? The sale had been made. Nothing Jenny said would change that.

Finally, after refusing a second drink, Jenny was able to escape.

She didn't get home until after eleven-thirty, and she felt bone-tired. No wonder. It had been a seventeen-hour day. She wasn't even sure she had the energy for the bath. Maybe she'd just crawl into bed.

She kicked off her pumps and walked into her minuscule office. The light on her answering machine was blinking. She pressed the button to play her messages.

"Hi, Jen, it's Simon. You there yet? Okay, guess not. Uh, it's ten o'clock, I called you at work but Pete said you'd gone. Call me when you get home, okay?"

The machine beeped, then another message started. Again she heard Simon's voice.

"Jenny? You home yet? No. Okay. Listen, it's nearly eleven and I guess I'll hit the sack. Just wanted to let you know I'm not going to be at the track tomorrow or Wednesday. I'm flying to Austin tomorrow morning at eight to meet with a prospective client, and then I'm going to spend the night with my folks in Georgetown. I won't be back until Wednesday sometime. But I thought if—'' The message stopped abruptly.

The machine beeped again.

''Stupid machine cut me off,'' Simon's voice said. ''Anyway, what I started to say is I wondered if you'd like to go see the Rockets play Wednesday night? If you want to, leave me a message. I'll call you when I get back on Wednesday.''

Jenny couldn't help smiling, even though she was still kind of ticked at Simon. But at least he'd *asked* her if she wanted to go to the game this time. She decided she would probably go. She'd actually thought about calling Simon this afternoon to tell him about the sale of the paper. Seeing him Wednesday night would be better, though. By then, Evan Armstrong would have arrived in Houston and held his first meeting with the staff, and she'd have even more to discuss with Simon.

''Okay, Simon,'' she said aloud. ''You're getting another chance. Don't blow it!''

Simon didn't mind admitting he was impressed when his rental car crested the hill and he got his first view of Hill Country Winery tucked into a sheltered valley. Acres and acres of neat rows of grapevines filled his vision, and as he got closer and rounded a curve in the two-lane road, he saw the winery itself— a cluster of several redbrick buildings.

He drove through the entrance and into the paved parking area. Earlier, Philippe Rousseau, the owner of the winery, had briefed Simon over the phone. ''Come to my office. The entrance is around the back of the wine shop building.''

Simon walked around the designated building and found the door marked Office.

A handsome dark-haired, dark-eyed older man turned from the filing cabinet as Simon entered the office. "Simon Christopher?" he said in a French-accented voice, walking forward with his right hand extended.

"Yes."

"Hello. I am Philippe Rousseau."

Simon shook Rousseau's hand. Rousseau asked him to be seated, and for the next thirty minutes, gave him a short history of Hill Country Wines. Simon learned that Rousseau had come to Texas from France more than fifteen years ago. "I was a young and cocky vintner," Rousseau explained. "I expected to immediately impress American wine makers." He smiled self-deprecatingly. "In my youth and arrogance, I had forgotten something important—it takes time to build a reputation."

Yet sometimes overnight, success did come to a business, Simon thought. His own was a prime example.

"I learned to be patient. To work and refine my product. And last year," Rousseau said with quiet pride, "for the first time, a Hill Country wine won a gold at the *Dallas Morning News* national. That's one of the nation's top ten wine competitions. And this year, we won two golds and a silver."

Even Simon, who knew only what he'd been able to cram into his head in a couple of nights of studying the business, knew winning two golds and a silver was very good.

"So now I believe we are finally ready to expand our marketing effort. That's why I'm looking for an advertising agency to represent us."

"Alonzo and Christopher would love to be that agency, Mr. Rousseau."

Rousseau went on to explain how he hoped to attract the lucrative thirty-something group of consumers. "I want advertising that is innovative and memorable. Something that will make the name Hill Country Wines stick in buyers' minds so that when they go to buy a bottle of wine, they will automatically ask for ours."

Simon could feel the stirring of excitement. This was the kind of product that would be fun to sell. He would be forever grateful to Western Oil, the corporation which had put Alonzo and Christopher on the map. Representing a large oil company trying to improve their image after several oil spills had been challenging, but it hadn't been fun.

In some ways, Simon could understand why Jenny had been so outspokenly disapproving of what he did for a living. Jenny was nothing if not an environmental nut. But she couldn't object to a winery as a client, could she? Jenny enjoyed a good glass of wine as much as the next person.

For the remainder of Simon's visit, Rousseau took him on a tour of the winery. First, they walked out to the closest field of grapevines.

"By the end of May, these flowers that you see will have turned into grape clusters," Rousseau explained. "They will grow throughout the summer."

"When are the grapes picked?" Simon asked. Although it wasn't necessary to know these things to plan an ad campaign, Simon had found that steeping himself in knowledge of the steps it took to bring a product to market helped him when he began the creative process of a campaign.

"When they are picked varies. Depending on the weather, the grapes mature at different speeds. We check to see that the proper sugar to acid ratio is reached, one that we feel will yield the balanced, flavorful wines we are known for. When it is, we will pick them."

Rousseau smiled. "Claude Junét, my head wine maker, will frequently be found in the vineyards, personally tasting the grapes to evaluate their flavor and maturity."

Simon thought how much Jenny would enjoy seeing all of this. Maybe, if he won the account, he could bring her up here some weekend.

"What happens then?" Simon asked.

"I'll show you when we get to the winery itself."

The largest building was where the wines were actually made and stored. Although the day was warm, almost hot, inside it was very cool, and Rousseau explained that to maintain that coolness, the walls of the building were over two feet thick.

He enthusiastically described the wine-making process, talking about Bucher presses, must chillers, advanced fermentation, French oak barrels, varietal wines and more. He showed Simon the cellars where the wines were aged, then led him back outside to the public tasting room.

"A wine should be judged by its appearance, smell, taste and finish," Rousseau said.

He showed Simon how to pour a small amount—half an inch to an inch—into a tasting glass, then hold it against a white, bright surface and evaluate its overall appearance—its color, clarity and viscosity.

Smiling, he demonstrated how Simon should swirl the wine in the glass several times, then put his nose into the glass and take a deep sniff. Then he instructed him in sipping, how to move the wine slowly across the palate.

"You should experience the taste of the wine on different parts of your tongue," Rousseau said. "Sweet on the tip, bitter at the back and acidity around the sides."

He talked about how to evaluate the flavor and dryness or sweetness of the wine, the body, tannin, acidity and intensity, how to take stock of its quality, whether or not it was balanced, whether the finish was short or lingering, whether the wine was complex.

By the time he was finished, Simon's head was swimming.

"I know, I know," Rousseau said, "I've told you far more than you could possibly absorb at one time. It's just that I'm so enthusiastic about our wines, and about wine making in general."

"It's a fascinating business," Simon agreed, thinking he'd enjoy learning more. "And you've given me some great insight into what goes into it."

For the rest of Simon's visit, Rousseau told him what he *didn't* want in an ad campaign. Finally, he said, "I'd like to see a presentation in two weeks. Can you have something ready by then?"

"Certainly." Alonzo and Christopher would have something ready if it killed them. "I'm assuming we're not the only agency you've contacted."

Rousseau smiled. "You are one of three in contention. The other two are New York agencies, but I'll be honest with you. I prefer to work with you. I like the idea of a local agency representing me, and if you can come up with an idea I like, the account will be yours."

When Simon left, he felt more excited than he had in a long time. This was the kind of challenge he'd been missing. He was looking forward to working up a presentation that would knock Rousseau's socks off. He could hardly wait to get back to Houston to get started.

Evan Armstrong was just as Jenny remembered him. Tall and rugged, with thick gray hair and piercing dark eyes. He assembled the entire staff in the sales department bull pen, and without wasting any time, launched into a forceful speech.

He told them about his personal history in the business, which Jenny already knew, about the financial position of his company and about his plans for the future.

"I hope to rival the Medlock-MacAllister chain," he said, naming the largest weekly newspaper conglomerate in the country. "And the acquisition of the *Vanguard* is an important step toward that goal."

He assured them, just as Gloria had, that he planned to make no changes in policy or personnel. "The only aspect of the paper that might change is the way the business itself is conducted, but that will be only after a careful study." He paused, looking around the room, meeting each person's gaze briefly. "To that end, I plan to bring in a general manager. I can't be here on a daily basis, and I don't believe in long-distance management."

Gloria smiled brightly the whole time he was speaking. She caught Jenny's eye toward the end. *See?* her expression said. *Didn't I tell you there was no reason to worry?*

Jenny did feel relieved. Armstrong inspired a feeling of confidence. And he seemed sincere about his lack of plans for change.

Still, that bit about a new general manager made Jenny wonder if her relief was premature. Perhaps she'd reserve judgment until she met this new general manager and saw for herself that things would remain the same.

One good thing about the sale of the paper, she thought that evening as she prepared for her outing with Simon—she refused to call it a date, knowing Simon didn't think of their evenings together that way—worrying about the future of the paper had successfully kept her from brooding over her unhappiness with her personal situation.

She stared into her closet.

Normally, she wore very conservative clothing—tailored dresses and suits, subdued colors, nothing flashy or frilly. She just wasn't the type. And when they went to the Rockets games, she wore blue jeans and her red Rockets T-shirt.

Tonight, though, she wanted to look different, make Simon really notice her.

From deep in her closet, she unearthed a jumpsuit her sister Cindy had given her last year for her birthday. Jenny had never worn it. But now she eyed it thoughtfully.

Should she?

The jumpsuit was a bold black-and-white stripe made out of some kind of silky material. The pants had deep pockets, and the top a V neck and wide collar. The belt was a wide black patent leather.

She held it up to her. You're being ridiculous, she thought. Do you think different clothes are going to make Simon think of you in a different way?

Disgusted with herself, she threw the jumpsuit on her bed and reached for her jeans. She was who she was.

She put on her jeans and T-shirt.

Simon's car pulled into the driveway right on the dot at seven. Jenny had been watching for him. She grabbed her purse and headed for the door. By the time she got there, he was standing on the stoop.

"Hi," he said.

He was dressed the way she was, in jeans and T-shirt, and she was glad she had resisted the urge to wear the jumpsuit. He would have probably thought she was nuts.

"Hi." She opened the screen door and walked outside, trying to ignore her traitorous heart, which had started pumping harder the minute she'd laid eyes on him.

Boy, she sure was a mess if she couldn't even look at Simon without getting all fluttery inside.

As they rode the short distance to the Summit, neither talked much. Jenny could feel Simon's eyes on her several times, but he didn't say anything, so she didn't, either. For the first time she could remember, she felt awkward with him, as if he were someone she didn't know.

Finally, as they pulled into the underground parking garage, she said, "Are Mark and Brooke going to be there tonight?"

"No. They had other plans. No one's using the other two tickets."

Jenny was glad. She knew it was selfish of her. She knew dozens of people who would have loved the free tickets, but tonight she didn't want to have to make small talk.

When they were settled into their second-row courtside seats, Jenny said, "How was your trip?"

Simon's eyes lit up. "It went well. We've been asked to make a presentation. Boy, I'd really like to get this account."

"Is it a big one?"

"No, it's not particularly big, at least not yet, but it's the kind of campaign we can sink our teeth into. And it'll be interesting." He grimaced. "And we sure as hell need something interesting. I've been bored silly lately."

"You? Bored?" Simon was never bored.

"I know. It's not like me. But now that we don't have to struggle like we did in the beginning, work isn't any fun. There's been no challenge."

"At least you don't have to worry about someone selling the agency out from under you," Jenny said bitterly.

Just then, the Rockets announcer began introducing the players, and the fans got very loud, so they had to quit talking. When the noise died down, Simon said, "That was an odd remark."

Jenny looked at him. "Gloria sold the paper."

Simon's eyes widened. "You're kidding."

"You know I wouldn't kid about something so serious."

He whistled. "Who did she sell to? And why?"

Jenny told him about Evan Armstrong and everything that had transpired since she'd last seen him on Saturday. She sighed. "I don't know... They both say there'll be no changes, but I'm worried. After ad revenue, editorial policy is the first thing a new owner looks at."

"So why is that bad?"

"Simon! You *know* why. The editorial policy of the *Vanguard* is something I believe in strongly. I don't want it to change."

A loud cheer erupted when the Rockets' center made a flashy, one-handed basket, and Simon jumped up and shouted, too. When he sat back down, and the crowd quieted a bit, he said, "Perhaps it's time for it to change."

"Why do you say that?"

"Well, to tell you the truth, I think the *Vanguard* could use some shaking up. I've always thought it takes itself too seriously. After all, it's just a neighborhood weekly. We're not talking the *New York Times* here."

Jenny bristled. "That's one of the stupidest things I've ever heard you say. You don't know what you're talking about."

"Well, pardon me," Simon said with exaggerated politeness. "I guess it's okay for you to make disparaging remarks about my business, of which you know nothing, but it's not okay for me to give my honest opinion of yours, is that it?''

Jenny glared at him. ''Are you comparing the *advertising* business with *journalism?* For your information, there *is* no comparison.''

''Oh, for Pete's sake, Jenny, lighten up, will you? As a matter of fact, the whole damned *paper* needs to lighten up. I, for one, would welcome some happy news once in a while.''

''Happy news!'' Jenny was outraged. ''I can't believe you said that!''

''What's not to believe? Personally, I'm tired of all the doom and gloom, and so are a lot of other people I know. Lord, to hear you people tell it, the sky is always falling.''

''We journalists have a duty to report what's happening in the world,'' Jenny said stiffly, ''whether people like it or not. Unlike you, I happen to think I have a responsibility to the public.''

''Meaning?''

''Meaning that persuading people to buy junk they don't need and can't afford or helping to whitewash some big oil company that has contributed to the devastation of our environment and our children's future isn't exactly admirable or responsible.''

Simon's jaw hardened, and his eyes narrowed.

Jenny swallowed. Maybe she'd gone too far this time.

''I'd like to remind you that advertising revenue is what allows your precious newspaper to exist. Just how long do you think you'd be around if businesses stopped advertising?''

"I—"

"And I just want you to know that your self-righteous, holier-than-thou attitude is really starting to get to me."

And with that, he turned away from her. Jenny knew he was right. She knew she'd overreacted to his earlier comments, and she wanted to say she was sorry, but the words stuck in her throat.

For the rest of the evening, they hardly talked. Simon kept his attention trained on the game and barely looked at her.

Jenny had never been more miserable. *What was happening to them?* she wondered. Before the past week, they had rarely argued. All of their debates had been good-natured and teasing, with an underlying consideration for each other's feelings.

Not so tonight.

Her entire life was falling apart around her.

Chapter Four

Jenny lay in bed and debated whether to skip her Thursday-morning run. The coward in her told her to stay home. She simply wasn't ready to face Simon...not yet. Justified or not, his digs the previous evening had hurt.

Self-righteous and holier-than-thou.

The words repeated themselves over and over in her mind. She squeezed her eyes shut.

Is that what he *really* thought of her?

Was she self-righteous and holier-than-thou? The images those words conjured weren't the kind she had ever imagined applied to her. She had always prided herself on her objectivity and open mind, her compassion and understanding.

Simon couldn't have meant what he'd said. He had just been striking back, reacting to her accusatory comments about his life's work. And, because she really was open-minded and fair, she had already admitted to herself that he had a right to be ticked off. To hit back.

That being the case, get your butt out of bed, and go meet Simon and tell him so. Don't let this argument fester one more day. The longer you put off seeing him and apologizing, the harder it's going to be.

She got up and hurriedly dressed for the track.

How would he act when she got there? she wondered. Last night, for the first time in years, he had not kissed her cheek or given her a hug when he'd left. He had simply said a cool good-night. He hadn't even made a reference to their morning run.

As she drove the short distance to the track, she prepared for possible scenarios by rehearsing several approaches. She wondered if he'd make it easy or hard for her.

Probably easy.

It wasn't in Simon to hold a grudge. In fact, it took a lot to get him angry in the first place.

Maybe he won't even be there.

But as she pulled into the parking lot, there was his Corvette parked in its usual spot. Trying to squelch the butterflies in her stomach, Jenny took a deep breath, got out of her car and walked over to the track.

The minute she saw Simon's face, she knew things were going to be all right.

"Jenny, I'm sorry," was the first thing he said. His eyes were a mirror image of her own, she knew, reflecting the same unhappiness and worry.

"I'm sorry, too."

He smiled then and put his arm around her, squeezing her shoulders. "I shouldn't have sloughed off your concern over the paper. I know this sale has rocked you."

"And I shouldn't have said what I did about your work. I—I didn't mean it."

He laughed suddenly. "Don't try convincing me you didn't mean it. I know you better."

Suddenly there was a lump in Jenny's throat. He was being awfully decent about this. "Maybe you're right," she said. "Maybe I *am* self-righteous."

"Aw, Jen, I shouldn't have said that. I was just mad at you." He squeezed her shoulders again. "C'mon." His voice was gentle. "Let's forget last night and get started, or you're going to be late for work."

She nodded, not trusting herself to speak, and they began their stretching exercises.

When their run was over, they walked out to the parking area. Simon stopped at his car and said, "Are you doing anything tonight?"

"Not that I know of."

"How about if I pick up a pizza and bring it over?"

Pleasure slid through her. "That sounds good."

He smiled, eyes warm as they rested on her face. "I'm glad you're not mad at me."

"Who said I'm not mad at you?"

He stared at her for a minute.

She tried to keep a straight face, but it was impossible.

When they waved goodbye, she was still grinning.

Jenny decided to defrost some brownies for their dessert—Simon loved brownies—and had just re-

moved them from the freezer, when Simon arrived
with the promised pizza.

"What kind did you get?" she asked as she set out
plates and poured iced tea.

"Cholesterol City Special," Simon said, eyes twin-
kling. "Loaded with two kinds of cheese, pepperoni,
sausage, bell peppers and mushrooms."

"Are you trying to kill me?" Jenny said with a
groan.

"But what a way to go." He dug into the box and
lifted a piece that was positively oozing fat.

"Mmm," Jenny said, taking a piece of her own and
biting into it. "This *is* good. Where did you get it?"

"That new place over on Rice Boulevard."

They ate companionably for a while, then Simon
said, "So when does the new general manager arrive?"

"I'm not sure. No one's said yet."

"Any word on who the person is?"

"Gloria told us today that his name is Bob Hennessey, and he's been working for Evan Armstrong for a
while." Jenny drank some iced tea. "Gloria doesn't
know him, so I guess we'll have to wait until he gets
here before we find out what he's like."

"How long is Gloria staying on?"

"Until Hennessey comes and they've had a chance
to go over some things."

"You still worried?"

Jenny nodded glumly. "I can't help worrying. I
know there will be changes. There are bound to be. I
just hope they're changes I can live with."

"The offer of a job at the agency is always open."

She rolled her eyes. "I know."

"Even if you want to use a job with us as a temporary kind of thing . . . you know . . . while you look for something else, you're still welcome."

"I really appreciate that, Simon." Although Simon's agency was the last place Jenny would want to work, it was generous of him to make the offer.

For a while, they talked about the new account he hoped to win. "You should see the winery, Jenny. The way you like to grow things, you'd love it."

"I didn't realize there were wineries so close to Austin," Jenny said, finishing off her third piece of pizza. She wiped her hands and mouth on her napkin and settled back into her seat with a satisfied sigh.

"Actually, neither did I." He reached for the last piece of pizza in the box. "If we, no, *when* we get the account, I'll take you up there to see it. We can spend the night at my parents' house."

Jenny nodded and smiled, but inwardly she cringed. Simon's parents were nice enough, she supposed, but the half-dozen or so times she'd been in their company, she hadn't felt comfortable. There wasn't anything concrete she could put her finger on, but she'd had the distinct impression they weren't as crazy about her friendship with Simon as he assumed—if he'd even thought about it—which, knowing Simon, he probably hadn't.

Simon had grown up in affluence. His father was a senior partner in Austin's largest and most prestigious law firm; his mother owned a small but exclusive art gallery and was a talented artist herself.

His sister Samantha, two years younger, had made her debut at the Daughters of the Confederacy ball and now held an enviable position as an assistant prosecutor with the Austin D.A.'s office.

Simon's parents played golf and duplicate bridge. They belonged to an expensive country club and lived in a gorgeous, antique-filled home in Georgetown, just north of Austin.

Jenny had a more humble background. Jenny's father was a retired mailman. Her mother worked as a public school secretary. Jenny was the only one in her family who had earned more than a high school education. Her parents still lived in the small frame house in Bellaire, an older section of Houston, where Jenny had grown up. Their leisure activities mostly consisted of her father watching sports on TV or tinkering around the house, and her mother making clothes for her grandchildren or gossiping on the phone.

Jenny figured that Simon's mother, in particular, probably worried that her friendship with Simon might turn into something more. And she was sure that would not please Leona Christopher. The Christophers undoubtedly felt their son could do much better.

Well, Jenny thought glumly, her pleasure in the evening fading, so far Simon's parents had nothing to worry about.

"Hey, you still with me?" Simon said.

"Oh, sorry, I guess I was daydreaming. What were you saying?"

Simon proceeded to relate a story about a client who had phoned him earlier in the day. He laughed as he told Jenny about the conversation. "We found the perfect person to pitch her company's barbecue sauce—Butch Bonner—the ex-Oilers' coach."

Jenny nodded. Bonner was perfect: a big, jovial good-old-boy type who obviously liked to eat and who had a nice, easy way about him.

"And she said no way," Simon continued. "When Mark asked her why she didn't want Bonner, she said she didn't like men named Butch." Simon rolled his eyes. "Can you believe it? Seems she used to be engaged to some joker named Butch who dumped her, and now she's got this completely illogical prejudice against anyone with that name. She said we'd have to find someone else." He shook his head. "I don't know *what* Bonner's going to say. I wouldn't be surprised if he sued us."

Jenny couldn't help chuckling, even though she understood Simon's frustration. "Didn't you try to reason with her?"

Simon shrugged. "Hell, what was the use? She's a woman. Women think with their emotions. To try to use logic on her would have been an exercise in futility."

Jenny's amusement vanished. "Excuse me? I'm a woman, and I think my mind is just as logical as any man's I've ever encountered."

"Oh, I know, but you're different. I never think of you as a woman."

The words hit Jenny like blows from a hammer. She stared at Simon. He was blithely eating a brownie, completely oblivious to how deeply his words had cut her. When long seconds ticked by in silence, he finally looked up.

"Boy, Simon," Jenny said, "you certainly know how to make a woman feel good about herself."

He blinked. "Huh?"

How could he be so dense? "I don't consider it a compliment that you never think of me as a woman."

"Aw, hell, Jenny," he said sheepishly, "I'm sorry. I didn't mean anything by what I said. You know that."

"Do I?" She was fighting tears, telling herself if she broke down and cried, she'd never be able to face him again. Never.

He stood and walked around the table. He leaned over and awkwardly put his arm around her. "Come on. It's just that you're my buddy. We've never had that man-woman thing between us."

"I know. It's okay."

But it wasn't okay.

And throughout the rest of the evening, Jenny forced herself to pretend everything was fine, but she couldn't stop thinking about what Simon had said, and she couldn't prevent feeling the hopelessness that nearly overwhelmed her. She couldn't wait for him to leave.

Finally, he did.

That night, Jenny couldn't fall asleep. Over and over, the words Simon had used played in her mind. He never thought of her as a woman. They'd never had that man-woman thing between them.

That was exactly the problem.

Jenny didn't want to be Simon's "buddy" any longer. She wanted him to see her and think of her as a desirable woman—a goal that now looked farther away than ever.

Jenny knew something had to change. She had been kidding herself that she and Simon could remain friends. It was becoming more clear every day that that was not going to be possible.

Tomorrow, she promised herself before falling into a troubled sleep. *Tomorrow I've got to come up with some kind of plan for the future. I can't go on this way.*

Becky had agreed to meet Jenny for lunch at Luby's Cafeteria on Kirby, which was right around the corner from Jenny's office.

"What's wrong? You sounded so funny over the phone," Becky said when they were seated at a corner table with their lunches in front of them.

Jenny looked at her sister. "I've got a serious problem, and I just had to talk to somebody about it."

Becky's eyes widened in alarm. "What? Jen, you're scaring me."

"Oh, it's nothing like that. I'm not dying, or anything." Then she laughed mirthlessly. "Unless someone can die of unrequited love."

Becky's mouth dropped open. "Uh, did I hear you correctly?"

Jenny sighed. "Yes. You heard me."

"It's Simon, isn't it?"

"Yes. It's Simon."

"I knew it! I just knew it. In fact, Cindy and Ma and I were talking about the two of you just the other day—"

"Cindy and Ma!" Jenny and her other sister weren't as close as she and Becky were. "Is everyone in the family *talking* about me? Oh, no," she moaned, "that's all I need."

"Everyone is not talking about you. Ma just mentioned that you hadn't brought Simon around lately, and then she said she knew you two were just friends, but she'd always hoped something else would develop between you, and Cindy said she couldn't imagine a platonic friendship between any woman and a guy with as much sex appeal as Simon has, and I said..." Becky stopped for breath, then continued. "I said I thought maybe there *was* an attraction there, but neither one of you had realized it yet."

"Ha! What a joke. He doesn't know I'm alive...not in that way, anyway," Jenny said miserably. She met her sister's sympathetic gaze. "And...oh, God, Becky, I'm so terribly in love with him. It's awful, and I don't know what to do about it."

Becky ate some of her fish. "Have you ever talked about this with Simon?"

"Talked about it! Are you crazy? How could we talk about it? I told you, he thinks of me as a buddy. A pal. Just like he does his male friends. If I said anything at all to give him a hint of the way I feel, that would be the end of our friendship."

Becky thought a moment, then said, "Seems to me that this friendship is standing in your way. Maybe putting an end to the friendship will open Simon's eyes."

"I don't think anything would open his eyes." Then Jenny repeated what Simon had said the previous evening. Her face twisted. "So you see how hopeless it is. Not only does he not think of me in romantic terms, he doesn't even think of me as a woman!"

"Oh, Jen," Becky said softly.

Jenny ate some of her salad and tried not to think what a hopeless case she was. She sighed deeply. "I don't know what to do," she said again. "I've gone over it and over it and I can't come up with a solution."

"The solution is to somehow force Simon to look at you in a different way," Becky said. "To think of you as a woman."

She ate more fish.

"The chances of that happening are about equal to my chances of winning the lottery."

Becky laughed. "Oh, come on, it's not *that* bad."

"No. It's worse."

"Okay, let's quit feeling sorry for ourselves," Becky said briskly, "and come up with a plan to get his attention."

"I've got it. I'll buy a pit bull and have him bite Simon. That'll certainly get his attention!"

Becky gave her a pained look.

Jenny sighed again. "Sorry. It's just that the whole thing is so hopeless."

"If you say the word 'hopeless' one more time, I'm going to smack you, Jenny."

"Fine. The situation isn't, you know, that word you dislike. It's . . . impossible."

Becky picked up the wadded paper from her packet of sweetener and threw it at Jenny. "Will you get serious?"

"I'm tired of being serious. I'm tired of being miserable, too."

"Okay, fine, give up," Becky said disgustedly. "If you want to be a quitter, why should I care?"

"I'm not a quitter."

"You're sure acting like one. You're also feeling sorry for yourself, and that's not like you, either."

Jenny's eyes filled with tears. "I'm sorry," she whispered.

Becky's face dissolved into sympathy. "No, I'm sorry. I know how you feel. I do. It's just that you've got to *do* something about it."

"How could you know how I feel?" Jenny said. "Heck, Jimmy proposed to you on your third date."

Becky looked at her for a long moment. "There was someone else. Someone before Jimmy."

"Becky! You never told me that."

"I know. Not many people know."

"Who was he?"

"That's not really important. He was someone I worked with before I met Jimmy, and I was crazy about him. Unfortunately, he was married."

"Becky!"

"I know. Awful, isn't it?"

"Did you know he was married when you . . . when you fell for him?"

Becky shook her head. "No, but that didn't make it any easier to bear." Then she sighed. "But back to your problem. The way I see it is . . . you have three possible options."

"Okay."

"Number one is you can do nothing, just remain friends with Simon the way you've been doing."

"I told you, Beck, I can't keep doing that. It's getting too hard. Sooner or later I'm going to give myself away."

"Okay. Number one is eliminated. Number two, you can get away from Simon completely. Move away from Houston."

Jenny nodded glumly. She'd already considered that.

"But number three is the one I favor," Becky added.

"What's that?"

"What I said before. Get his attention."

"And how am I supposed to accomplish that miracle?"

"Well, there are several ways to go about it. The first would be to change your appearance and the way you behave. Get him to see you in a different light."

"You mean like dye my hair blond, or something?" Jenny said suspiciously.

"No, nothing so drastic. Just, you know, get a different hairstyle, something more sexy, and jazz up your wardrobe. You know, get some sexier, more feminine clothes."

"I knew it. I'm dull and boring."

"Jenny, don't twist what I'm saying. You're *not* dull and boring, but Simon is used to you this way. He'll never look at you in another way unless you somehow change."

"I don't think I can do what you're suggesting."

"Of course you can."

"I'd feel ridiculous. I suppose you think I should start wearing short skirts and low-cut blouses."

"Not necessarily, but would it kill you to buy a red dress, for example, and to do something exciting with your hair. You've worn that same hairstyle since you were in high school, for heaven's sake."

"I *am* boring."

Becky rolled her eyes. "And if that doesn't do it, you could always try to make him jealous."

If Jenny hadn't been feeling so completely pathetic, she might have laughed. "That cliché? Make him jealous?"

"Yes. Believe me, it works. Why do you think things like that are called clichés? Because they're tried-and-true, that's why."

Jenny shook her head. "Look, Beck, I appreciate your concern and your ideas, and I'm grateful that you listened to me, but I can't do what you're suggesting. It's fake. It's not me. I do have some pride, you know."

Becky shrugged. "Fine. See how much company your pride is after Simon finally finds someone else to marry."

Becky's arrow hit its mark. For the rest of the day, every time Jenny thought of Simon married to someone else, she felt as if that arrow were firmly wedged right in the middle of her heart.

Chapter Five

Simon had been killing himself for a week—coming up with idea after idea for Hill Country Wines.

None of them was any good.

He'd exhausted every possibility. He and Mark and the rest of the staff had brainstormed until the wee hours of several mornings.

Nothing suitable emerged.

Everything had been done before. Nothing was fresh or exciting or gave Simon that feeling in the pit of his stomach—the one that said they had a winner.

He didn't know what they were going to do. They were no closer to a presentation for Philippe Rousseau than they had been the day Simon returned from his visit to the winery. Farther away, in fact, for in the beginning Simon had been all fired up about the prospective account.

Now all he felt was discouraged.

Seven days gone and nothing to show for them.

In just seven more days, they were supposed to present their ideas to Rousseau.

"So what are we going to do?" Mark said.

"I don't know," Simon said. He picked a piece of lint from the trousers of his dark gray suit, then propped his long legs up on his desk and leaned back in his chair.

"We could always go with the offbeat celebrity endorsement," Mark suggested.

"There's nothing new about that."

Mark nodded wearily and subsided into silence. The onyx clock on Simon's credenza struck the hour, the chimes echoing through the room.

Simon swung his legs down, stood and walked to the broad expanse of window. He stared out. Twenty floors below, the traffic on Westheimer crawled along. It was five o'clock. Rush hour.

He ran his hands through his hair in frustration. Turning, he said, "Listen, Mark, I'm bushed. I can't see that we're going to get anything productive done by sitting here staring at each other. Why don't we both go home, get a good night's rest and call a staff meeting for eight tomorrow morning? We can hash over everything we've come up with so far. Maybe we've missed something."

Mark sighed. He looked as tired as Simon felt. "Okay. I'll tell everyone." He gave Simon a rueful smile. "Brooke won't believe it when she comes home and I'm actually there to have dinner with her."

Simon thought about Mark going home to Brooke and wished he had someone to go home to. Someone whose shoulder he could cry on. Someone who would commiserate with him and understand his frustration.

He wearily cleared his desk of papers. He was supposed to attend a fraternity alumni meeting tonight, but he decided he would pass. Instead, he would go home, fix a sandwich or two, have a couple of beers and do nothing that required any brainpower.

Jenny awakened early Wednesday to the sound of rain. Hard rain. She groaned, got up and peered through the slats of the miniblinds to the street beyond. Rain sluiced the window, and she could hardly see out.

No running this morning, she thought. Well, she'd just go into the office early. Bob Hennessey, the new general manager, was scheduled to arrive today—his first day on the job, and Jenny wanted to be prepared.

She was nervous about meeting him. If only she knew what to expect.

As she showered and dressed, she thought about how out of control everything in her life seemed to be. Her job. Her love life.

Then she laughed aloud. Love life! Her love life was nonexistent.

Her thoughts drifted to Simon. She hadn't seen much of him the past week or so. She knew he was working on a new campaign, so he'd been spending a lot of time at his office. That suited her. She had needed the time away from him to think.

Not that her thinking had done her any good. She had just gone around in circles, always arriving back at the same place.

But at least not seeing much of him had relieved some of her tension. Maybe her life *would* be better if she moved away from Houston, she thought now.

Gathering up her purse, a plastic rain parka, her umbrella and her keys, she prepared to leave. Well, today's meeting with Bob Hennessey might give her some answers. If things didn't look good for her at the paper, she just might not have any choice but to leave Houston.

She went out the back door, locking it carefully behind her. Although the house, which her great-aunt Jenny had bought over fifty years ago, was old and didn't offer much in the way of modern conveniences, it did have a covered walkway between the house and the single-car garage.

Jenny said a prayer of thanks. Without the protection of the walkway, she would have been soaked before ever getting into her car. And that would not have been a good way to start the day.

Especially this day.

Jenny's garage had a garage-door opener, a gift from her father for her thirtieth birthday. She pressed the button to open the door, then climbed into her car and dumped her belongings on the passenger seat.

She turned the key in the ignition, then tried to push the gearshift into reverse. It wouldn't move. She looked down, wondering what she was doing wrong. She tried to shift again. It wouldn't budge. It was as if the gears were frozen.

Oh, no!

Jenny closed her eyes. Why was this happening, today of all days?

If it can happen, it will.... Jenny's mother was always spouting truisms, especially Murphy's Law. Lois Randall was a cheerful pessimist, a living oxymoron, as Jenny once laughingly described her.

This morning, Jenny wasn't laughing.

Ten minutes later, as she waited for her neighborhood mechanic to show up, she dug her savings passbook out of her desk and looked at the pitiful balance. Less than a thousand dollars. If anything major was wrong with her car, the cost of repairs was going to wipe her out.

Maybe it's something really simple. Some little glitch. Oh, please, God, let it just be a little glitch.

When Felix, the mechanic, arrived, he dashed her hopes. "I think it's the transmission. I'll have to tow it in and give you a call later."

Jenny nodded stoically. *What will be will be.* That was another of Lois Randall's irrefutable declarations.

After Felix had gotten her car hooked up to his tow truck and driven off with it, Jenny went inside to call Megan, the advertising manager and her closest friend at the paper, to ask her for a lift to work.

Unfortunately, Megan must have had the same idea as Jenny about going in early today, because all Jenny got was her friend's answering machine.

If the day had been nice, Jenny could have walked to work. It was only about ten blocks. But there was no way she was walking in this downpour.

That left Simon. She knew he wouldn't mind giving her a ride to work.

"Sure," he said in a sleep-fogged voice. "You in a hurry? Do I have time for a cup of coffee first?"

"Well, I had hoped to get to the office early today. The new general manager's supposed to be there."

"Oh, yeah, I forgot." He yawned. "I'll be there in five minutes."

"I'll be watching for you."

Jenny waited under the overhang in front, and darted out to the sidewalk when she saw his car. He leaned over to open the passenger door, and she gratefully sank inside. "Thanks, Simon. I really appreciate this."

He grinned. "Good. That means you owe me." He backed the car out of the driveway and shifted. "I don't do this for just anyone."

Jenny's heart tripped as her gaze took him in. His hair was still tousled from sleep, and he'd obviously hurriedly thrown on a pair of nylon running shorts topped by a rumpled white T-shirt. His bare feet were thrust into beat-up moccasins. She swallowed hard, as a sudden picture of Simon in bed, his lean, tanned body sprawled across tangled sheets, filled her mind. Warmth stole through her body as she tore her gaze away from the enticing image she'd conjured.

"What's wrong with your car?" he said.

She shrugged. "I won't know until Felix has a chance to look at it in the shop." She heaved a sigh. "God, I hope it's nothing serious."

"Yeah," he said sympathetically.

Jenny glanced at him and he gave her an encouraging smile. She knew he'd never had to worry about money the way she did, yet he did seem to understand.

"It just seems like everything's going wrong," she said. "My job, the car..." *And my hopeless love for you.* She pushed the thought away. She had enough to worry about today. She didn't need to start thinking about Simon again.

When he pulled up in front of her building, he said, "Will you need a ride home?"

"If I do, someone from the paper can take me."

"Well, good luck today. With the new boss, and all."

"Thanks."

She opened the door and stuck her umbrella out, trying to get it open before she had to climb out of the car. Just then, a loud rumble of thunder shook the air, followed by a sharp crack of lightning.

When it rains, it pours. Jenny laughed. She was beginning to think like her mother. And wasn't *that* alarming?

"Listen, Jen," Simon said as she got out. "Call me and let me know what Felix says, okay?"

"Oh, Simon, you've got your own problems."

"No. I mean it. Let me know what he says."

"All right. I will. Thanks again for the ride."

He waved away her thanks and took off as she headed into the building.

Bob Hennessey was a shock—tall, blond and astonishingly good-looking. He was dressed in what looked to Jenny like an Armani suit paired with a collarless black shirt and soft European leather loafers.

All the female employees seemed tongue-tied in the face of this elegant, sophisticated man, who seemed completely out of place in the casual, low-paid atmosphere of a small weekly newspaper.

Jenny, who hadn't been feeling overly self-confident lately, felt even less so in her inexpensive beige summer suit and plain white blouse. Only Gloria, who loved designer clothes, was a match for him in her red linen dress and red-and-white spectator pumps.

Jenny had instructed Carla, the receptionist, to take a message if Felix called during the staff meeting. She didn't want Hennessey's first impression of her to be of someone who took personal calls during important staff meetings.

Not that he'd said much of any importance, she thought as the meeting finally drew to a close just before lunchtime. He had simply parroted everything said earlier by Evan Armstrong and Gloria. He did promise to meet with each department head on an individual basis over the next week. "Just to orient me," he said smoothly.

Uh-huh, Jenny thought. Like you won't be evaluating us, too.

As she headed back to her office, Carla beckoned to her. "Your mechanic called." She handed Jenny a pink telephone-message slip.

Jenny said a quick prayer as she dialed the number.

"Afraid I've got some bad news, Miss Randall," Felix said a few minutes later. "You need a new transmission."

"How much?"

"It's gonna cost you right around six hundred dollars."

Jenny's heart sank. Six hundred dollars. That would leave very little in her emergency fund. She closed her eyes wearily.

"Miss Randall? You still there?"

Sighing, she said, "Yes, Felix, I'm here."

"Should we go ahead and do the work?"

"Do I have another choice?"

"Not really."

"So do the work. When do you think it'll be finished?"

"We'll try to have it for you by five or six tomorrow afternoon. If not, it might be Monday."

Oh, great.

After Jenny hung up the phone, she sat staring into space for a few minutes, then, remembering her promise to Simon, she called his office.

"Hey," he said, "what's up?"

She told him.

"I'm sorry."

"It's not your fault."

"I know, but I'm still sorry. Listen, we'll probably work until at least seven, but how about if I take you someplace nice for dinner tonight? I need a break, myself."

"I have a better idea. You're always feeding me. Why don't you let me feed you for a change? I'll fix dinner at my place."

"Tell you what. Let's compromise. I'll pick up a couple of steaks and you can make the stuff to go along with them."

He was so sweet.

Why did he have to be so sweet? Why couldn't he be a jerk so she wouldn't love him anymore? Jenny's eyes suddenly filled with tears. Angrily, she brushed them away. What was wrong with her? Lately, she was crying at the drop of a hat.

"Now, what about a ride home?"

"Don't worry about me. I'll get a ride from someone here."

"Okay. I'll see you about seven-thirty."

Megan offered to give Jenny a ride home. "What's the matter, Jenny?" she said as they emerged from the building into tentative sunshine. The rain had finally stopped about an hour earlier, and the clouds were beginning to disperse. "You seem awfully down."

"I know. I'm sorry."

"It's more than your car troubles, isn't it?"

Jenny looked at Megan, who was unlocking the passenger door of her Mazda. "I'm worried about the paper. Aren't you?"

"Hey, what's the sense in worrying?"

Jenny got in the car and waited until Megan was in before saying, "You sound like my mother."

Megan smiled, her hazel eyes warm. "I learned a long time ago not to expend energy worrying about things over which I have no control."

"I can't help it. So much is at stake here. What if Hennessey makes drastic changes?"

"So we'll adapt."

Jenny sighed. Megan was so sensible. She made it all sound so easy.

"Sometimes you just have to roll with the punches."

"I don't want things to change," Jenny wailed. Megan braked for a red light. Turning to Jenny, she said, "Change isn't always bad, you know. Usually, when one door closes, another opens."

"I know, but it isn't just me I'm worried about. The *Vanguard* has always stood for something. That's what I'd hate to see change."

"If it does, it does," Megan said philosophically. "It won't be the end of the world." Megan smiled to soften her words. "You've got to stop taking things so seriously. Try to keep it all in perspective. I mean, we're not talking world peace here."

That was what Simon had said. "But what if Hennessey decides to eliminate your job? That could happen, you know."

Other weeklies that Jenny knew of combined the position of general manager and advertising manager. And Megan was self-supporting.

Megan shrugged. "It's out of my control. If it happens, I'll cope."

"I admire your attitude, but I'm afraid worrying is in my nature. So many people at the paper will be devastated if they lose their jobs."

Megan smiled kindly. "You're too young to be so intense, Jenny. You've got to learn to loosen up a little, take the time to enjoy your life and the good things God gave us. It's not your responsibility to shoulder the problems of the world."

After Megan had dropped her off at home, Jenny wondered if everyone thought she was a prig. Her spirits sank even lower.

She dumped her umbrella in the umbrella stand, walked into her bedroom and tossed her belongings onto her bed, then walked to the full-length mirror in the corner. She stared at herself—her feet in their sensible pumps, her neutral-colored stockings, her skirt which sedately covered her knees, her dull suit, her dull blouse, her dull hair.

No wonder Simon wasn't interested in her. No wonder he never thought of her as a woman. Why should he? She was dull and boring and not the least bit glamorous.

Megan had been kind when she'd said Jenny was too intense. What she'd probably meant to say was that Jenny's sense of humor had deserted her.

Oh, God, is that true? Have I turned into one of those horrible, humorless women who takes everything so seriously, she bores people to death?

She vowed then and there that she would change. She had to change. Even if Simon never fell in love with her the way she dreamed, she didn't want him to think of her the way she was afraid he was beginning to.

I'll start tonight, she promised herself. *I'll be open-minded and relaxed and I won't insult his career and I won't be glum and miserable.*

She felt better already.

Simon was determined to take Jenny's mind off her troubles. He was also determined to help her financially, one way or another.

Over the years, he had often felt guilty because he had never had financial worries of the kind Jenny had had to endure. That was one of the reasons that he always insisted on paying for the meals they ate out together or refused to take money for the food he brought to her house.

Jenny was proud, and she tried to pay her share. Sometimes he let her, especially when that particular evening hadn't been expensive to begin with.

Simon knew he was lucky. His family, while not wealthy, were extremely comfortable.

Jenny's family, while not poor, had to watch their pennies.

Even their college days had been from opposite ends of a pole. Simon had had a luxurious condo and a new car to drive, even during his freshman year.

Jenny had been at UT on a full scholarship and had had to work part-time for her spending money.

If Jenny was more serious about things than Simon, it was for good reason. Her life had been harder; she'd had to work harder for everything.

Simon admired Jenny more than he'd ever been able to tell her. The sixteen months she'd spent living with her great-aunt and nursing her through a long bout of cancer were typical of the loyalty and commitment she lavished on the people and issues she cared about.

Simon wondered if he would have acquitted himself half so well if he'd had to contend with the same kinds of obstacles and problems.

As he got out of his car and walked up to Jenny's door, he told himself he would cheer her up if it killed him.

But when she opened the door, she didn't seem unhappy at all. There was a smile on her face and in her eyes.

"I'm disappointed," Simon said.

"Why?"

"I thought I was going to have to cheer you up, but you already look cheerful."

She grinned, and he thought, not for the first time, that she had one of the prettiest smiles he'd ever seen. It was completely natural, just as she was. Simon liked that about Jenny. There was never any subterfuge. He always knew exactly what she was thinking and feeling.

"Sorry about that." She slid her face into a mock frown. "I'll try to be unhappy for your sake."

He joined in her laughter and followed her into the kitchen. As he entered the brightly lit room, he noticed for the first time that she looked different. When she turned around, he realized the difference was that she was wearing something totally unlike anything he'd ever seen her in before. It was a black-and-white striped jumpsuit, and it made her look...sexy.

The thought jolted him.

To cover his confusion, he handed her the steaks.

"Wow," she said, unwrapping the two thick sirloin strips—his favorite. "You went all out, didn't you?"

He was still thinking about her uncharacteristic clothing and his reaction to it. He shrugged. "What are you making to go along with them? I skipped lunch today, so I'm starved."

"French-fried onion rings, mushrooms and fresh green beans."

They worked alongside each other as they prepared the meal. When the mushrooms and green beans were ready, Jenny turned her attention to making the French-fried onion rings and Simon put the steaks in the broiler.

"What's that you're using for batter?" he asked. He liked cooking. He'd often thought, when he retired, he'd take up cooking.

"Pancake mix."

"Really?"

"Yeah," Jenny said. "Megan gave me that idea."

"How *is* Megan?" Simon asked.

Jenny used a serrated spoon to remove several onion rings from the hot oil. She laid them carefully on a paper-towel-covered plate. "She's fine."

"She worried about the changeover?"

"No. Megan doesn't waste her time worrying." Jenny smiled ruefully. "She lectured me today about that very thing, and she's right."

Simon nodded. "I wish I could stop worrying about the winery account we're trying to get."

Jenny put several more onion rings in the oil, which sizzled and spattered. "What's the problem?"

"We can't come up with anything innovative. I'm about to give up."

"You? You're not a quitter."

Simon turned the steaks. "While we eat, I'll tell you about the things we've come up with and blown off. Maybe you'll have some ideas for me."

"Okay."

They turned their attention back to the food. True to his word, Simon briefed Jenny on the Hill Country Wines campaign or lack thereof during their meal.

Jenny listened quietly, her dark eyes thoughtful. When he finished, she said, "Hmm. You really *have* exhausted a lot of possibilities, haven't you?"

"Afraid so." Recounting everything they'd thought of and rejected made Simon feel gloomy, and he reminded himself that it wasn't his problems they were supposed to be solving tonight. It was Jenny's. "But listen, it's okay. I don't expect you to have a solution.

I guess I just wanted to say it all out loud. Let's talk about you."

Jenny frowned. "No, let's not. I'm sick of thinking about myself. Besides, I thought of some—" She bit her bottom lip. "No, forget it."

"What?"

She hesitated. "I don't know, maybe this is stupid."

"Nothing is stupid when you're brainstorming."

She smiled. "Is that what we're doing?"

"If you've got an idea for me, that's what we're doing."

"Well," she said slowly, "as much as I hate to admit it, people really love soap operas. And what are soap operas except ongoing stories about people whose lives the viewers get caught up in? What if your campaign for Hill Country Wines centers on a young married couple and the special occasions in their lives?"

She was obviously thinking out loud now, her voice had taken on a dreamy quality. Simon could feel a tug of excitement in his gut.

"Something like *Hill Country Wine—the perfect way to celebrate those special occasions.* You could start out with your first commercial showing the man going into a wine shop and saying he needs something special because he's going to propose to his girlfriend that night. The clerk could say he has the perfect choice—a bottle of Hill Country Wine." Her eyes shone with excitement, an excitement that matched Simon's.

Simon stared at her. "I like it! No, I *love* it! Then the next frame could show him pouring her the wine, and she could say something like, 'What's the occasion?' and him smiling and presenting her with the ring."

Jenny grinned. "Then the rest of the campaign could unfold their story little by little. Having dinner with her folks and telling them they're engaged..."

"Having dinner with his parents and telling *them*," Simon said.

"The rehearsal dinner..."

"The wedding..."

"Their first dinner party..."

"Celebrating their first anniversary..."

"Patching up their first fight!" Jenny crowed in delight.

"His first promotion!" Simon echoed.

Jenny stopped, a big grin lighting her face. "And culminating in her telling him she's pregnant with their first baby!"

"And she could say, 'I sure am going to miss my Hill Country Wine.'" He jumped up, grabbed Jenny and twirled her around the room.

She laughed, her eyes sparkling with delight.

"You're a genius!" he shouted. "A genius!"

And then he kissed her, not on the cheek, the way he usually did, but full on her mouth, which was partway open.

The minute his mouth covered hers, and he felt the sweetness of her lips, the moist warmth of her mouth, the tip of her tongue and the soft curves of her body in the silk jumpsuit, something powerful erupted inside Simon.

Something besides the excitement of her idea.

And he recognized what that powerful feeling was.

Desire.

Chapter Six

Simon's kiss was so completely unexpected that Jenny had no time to engage her normal defenses.

The instant his mouth connected with hers, a torrent of emotions engulfed her, and all rational thought disappeared. Her knees turned to water, her head spun and a sweet elation spiraled through her. She clung to him as she poured all of her pent-up feelings into an instinctive and total response.

When Simon eventually released her, Jenny was still so stunned by the kiss, it took her a few moments to come back to earth and reality.

She grabbed hold of the table to steady herself. She still felt too tremulous from the dizzying aftermath of emotions assaulting her to be able to stand without support.

He seemed just as shaken as she. His breathing was uneven, and as their gazes met briefly, the knowledge of what had passed between them vibrated in the air.

"Y-you've saved my life," Simon said, his voice gruff. He grinned at her, but his eyes reflected the same confusion she was feeling.

Jenny laughed in an attempt to dilute some of the tension. "You told me I owed you one this morning," she said lightly. "Now we're even." Was he going to mention the kiss? Jenny's heart was still beating too hard, and her mouth tingled with the imprint of his lips.

"I don't think so," he said. "It's the other way around. I'm probably going to owe you for the rest of my life. Mark's gonna love your idea, and I think the client will, too."

"I'm glad." He wasn't going to mention it. He was just going to pretend the kiss hadn't happened. But it had. And he was thinking about it. She could see the awareness in his eyes, in the way he was carefully avoiding her gaze. She would have given anything to know exactly what his thoughts were right now.

He casually moved away from her, picked up his dinner plate and utensils and walked over to the counter. He rinsed his plate, then opened the dishwasher, his back to her the whole time, so she couldn't see his expression. "This is a very ambitious campaign we've mapped out," he said. "It's going to take a lot of work to get it together." He finally turned around, his blue eyes clear, his gaze direct. "I don't suppose you'd consider helping us prepare the presentation?"

"Me?" She, too, began clearing the table. Obviously, he had gotten himself under control. Okay. If he could pretend, so could she. "What could I do to help?"

"Lots of things, but mainly working with me on the copy for the commercials."

"But you have people on staff to do that, don't you?"

"No one as good as you."

She flushed with pleasure at the compliment.

"How about it?" he pressed. "Do you think you can set aside your prejudice about advertising long enough to help? We'd make it worth your while."

His offer was tempting. She could certainly use some extra money. And she did feel proprietary about the idea. It would be fun to see it come to fruition. And hadn't everyone been counseling her to loosen up, have more fun?

"But I have a day job. The only time I'd have to work for you is nights and weekends."

"I know. That's not a problem."

"Well . . ."

"C'mon, Jenny. Say yes."

She hesitated another moment or so, then, smiling, she met his gaze. "Yes."

He grinned. "Good. We'll start tomorrow night."

They finished cleaning up the kitchen as if it were a normal evening, just as if the kiss had never taken place, just as if things were the same as they'd always been. Yet the whole time they worked, Jenny kept thinking about the kiss and about her agreement to work with Simon on the Hill Country Wines campaign.

In the next few days, they would be together even more than they usually were. Was she crazy?

The butterflies in the pit of her stomach told her she must be. *Don't attach too much importance to that kiss. Don't expect it to happen again.*

Who was she kidding? That was exactly what she was hoping.

When they were nearly finished cleaning up the kitchen, she quit worrying about the upcoming weeks and began to worry about what would happen when he left tonight.

Would he kiss her cheek?

Would he finally say something about the kiss they had exchanged earlier?

And if he did, what would she say in return?

She needn't have worried.

When he left, he just gave her a quick hug and said he'd call her the next day to set up a time for them to begin work.

Later, Jenny lay in bed and replayed the entire evening in her mind, especially the kiss.

What had it meant?

That the kiss was different from any he'd ever given her before hadn't been her imagination.

It *had* been different.

Just thinking about it, remembering how it had felt to have his arms around her, his mouth covering hers, made her stomach feel as if the bottom had dropped out—exactly the same way she felt when she looked down from a great height.

Why had he kissed her like that? She knew he hadn't meant to. He had grabbed her in exuberance, in celebration and excitement over the idea they'd hatched together.

So what had happened?

Even though she continued to caution herself, she couldn't stop the tiny seedling of hope that had taken root.

Maybe her love for Simon wasn't as hopeless as she'd thought. Maybe he *did* feel something for her, something more than friendship.

She hugged her pillow and squeezed her eyes shut. Wordless prayers formed in her mind.

It was long after midnight before she fell into a restless sleep.

Simon couldn't understand what had happened to him tonight. He had kissed Jenny hundreds of times, but he had never felt the way he felt tonight.

All the other kisses had been given in affection. There had never been anything remotely like desire between them.

Tonight, all that had changed.

Tonight, something had ignited between them.

He had kissed her the way he kissed a woman he wanted sexually. And damn! He *had* wanted her. He hadn't wanted to break the kiss. He had been totally turned on.

The realization was alarming.

As he prepared for bed that night, he lectured himself. This was Jenny he was dealing with. His friend. His best friend. His best friend who trusted him.

You've been without a woman too long, and you'd better cool it.

Introducing a sexual element into his relationship with Jenny would be disastrous. It would completely ruin their friendship. And if Simon doubted it, he only had to look at the total absence of friendship between him and any of his ex-girlfriends.

But you were never friends with them to begin with.

Well, that was true, but the fact was, he and Jenny *were* friends, and he'd be crazy to do anything to jeopardize that friendship. It meant too much to him. He would do anything necessary to safeguard that relationship.

He punched up his pillow and determinedly closed his eyes. He would forget about tonight. Not only that—he would make sure nothing like that kiss happened again. Ever.

On Thursday morning when Jenny arrived at work, she was taken aback to see Bob Hennessey sitting behind Gloria's desk looking as comfortable as if he had been there for months.

"Good morning," she said, stopping by the open doorway.

He looked up and smiled, his perfect teeth looking as though they belonged in a toothpaste ad. "Good morning."

"You're an early bird."

He nodded. "I like early morning."

"I do, too." She smiled, then turned away, intending to go on down the hall to her office.

"Uh, Jenny... It *is* Jenny... right?"

His voice stopped her, and she looked back at him. "That's right."

"And you're the editor."

"Right again."

"Well, Jenny, I intend to start meeting with the department heads today, and since you're the first one here, why don't we get together and talk for a while?"

Jenny smothered a sigh. She wasn't sure she was prepared to meet with Hennessey just now, but she guessed she really didn't have a choice. "Let me get a cup of coffee first," she said. "And get rid of this stuff." She indicated her briefcase and sack lunch.

He smiled his agreement.

Five minutes later, Jenny faced him across Gloria's desk. "Is Gloria coming in today?" she asked.

"Yes, but she had an appointment this morning."

Jenny nodded. She sat quietly. This was his show.

"I've been reading your work," Hennessey said. "It's very good."

"Thank you." Jenny sipped her coffee.

"I especially like your editorials."

Jenny smiled. Writing the editorial was the high point of each week.

He tented his hands and studied her thoughtfully. "You have, how many, two assistant editors?"

"One assistant editor and one editorial assistant." Jenny wondered if his eyes really were that shade of aquamarine or if he wore colored contact lenses. The color was so unusual, she couldn't imagine that it was real.

"And the difference is?"

Jenny gave him a wry smile. "The difference is that the editorial assistant is a college student who only works part-time." And makes barely more than minimum wage, she wanted to add. She'd been pushing for a raise for Kim for months. The kid was really good, and she deserved it. But editorial was always last on the totem pole. Jenny knew the situation wasn't unique to the *Vanguard*. Would-be journalists were a dime a dozen.

He nodded and picked up his coffee. "I noticed that each issue of the paper contains a Business of the Week feature. Does your staff write those articles?"

Jenny tried not to grimace. "Yes."

"I take it you're not overly enthusiastic."

"I'm not thrilled about giving up editorial space, no, but I realize those features are a necessary evil since we depend so heavily on the goodwill of our advertisers."

In answer, he just nodded and sipped his coffee. His eyes over the rim of the cup were thoughtful.

Jenny wondered what he was thinking behind that perfect facade. She also wondered if she should have been more guarded in her answer. After all, she didn't know what his philosophy might be.

Well, it was better to get their cards on the table. She was not in favor of advertising-driven stories, and the sooner he realized it, the better, because she wasn't about to change her stance. She had agreed to the weekly feature, and had scrupulously covered the ribbon cuttings and grand openings, but that was the extent of her willingness to compromise.

"In some markets," he said, "we've instituted personal ads... quite successfully."

"Personal ads? You mean 'single white female wants to meet single white male' kind of thing?"

"Yes." He set down his coffee cup and leaned forward, resting his arms on the desk. "In Orange

County, we were able to raise advertising revenues by more than twenty percent.''

''Is that what you envision for the *Vanguard?*''

He shrugged. ''Right now, I'm planning no changes.''

''But you're considering something like personal ads.''

''I'm not closing the door on anything for the future.''

Jenny formulated her words carefully. ''Tell me, Mr. Hennessey—''

''It's Bob,'' he said, interrupting.

''Bob,'' she repeated.

He smiled, his perfect teeth and his perfect tan and his perfect eyes all presenting a perfectly pleasant picture. ''Yes.''

''All right. Tell me, Bob, do you come from an editorial background or an advertising background?''

The smile never slipped. ''Before coming to work for Evan Armstrong, you mean?''

''Yes.''

''I was advertising manager for the *Los Angeles Sentinel.*''

In that moment, Jenny knew it was a good thing she had the work with Simon's agency to fall back on if her job at the paper suddenly soured completely, because right now, things did not look good.

''And you say this was Jenny's idea?'' Mark said.

''Yes. Great, isn't it?'' Simon said. If anything, he felt more enthusiastic about her idea this morning than he'd felt last night.

Mark nodded. "It's perfect. Now, if only Philippe Rousseau thinks so."

"If he doesn't, then he's hopeless, and nothing we come up with will please him."

"How many episodes do you think we can have ready before we make our presentation?" Mark asked.

"Since we've only got a week, we'll be lucky to get two done, but I'd like to have three." Simon played with his pen. "Jenny's going to help write the copy."

Mark grinned. "How did you manage to arrange that?"

"It wasn't easy." The answer was automatic, the one Mark would expect.

But after Mark left, Simon, for the first time, realized it hadn't been difficult at all to persuade Jenny to help with the campaign. He wondered what had brought about her change of heart. Did the kiss have anything to do with it?

He immediately discarded that idea. She had been just as discomfited by that kiss as he'd been. Why else had they both pretended it hadn't happened? No, something had caused a transformation in her thinking even before that explosive kiss.

What was going on?

Jenny rushed home to change clothes before heading for Simon's office. She got there about six-thirty and was surprised to find only Simon and Mark still there, and Mark was obviously on his way out.

"Hi, Mark," she said.

"Long time no see," he said, giving her a big smile and a hug. "I've missed you."

"Thanks. I missed you, too." She liked Mark Alonzo and his wife, Brooke. They were lots of fun, but more than that, they were real people. Neither put on airs or acted as if they thought they were better than she was, even though they had a lot more money and lived a more sophisticated life-style.

"All right," Simon said, smiling, "cut out the mushy stuff. We have work to do."

Jenny made a face. "Slave driver."

"Better watch him," Mark said. "He uses a whip to keep our staff in line."

"He doesn't scare me," Jenny said.

Mark grinned and they made small talk for a few more minutes, then he said, "Well, if I don't get a move on, I'm going to be late, and Brooke hates to be kept waiting." He hugged Jenny again. "Thanks for saving our behinds, Jenny. If you hadn't come up with this idea for Hill Country Wines, we wouldn't have had a prayer of landing the account."

Once Mark was gone and she no longer had a buffer, shyness attacked Jenny. For a few seconds, she couldn't think of anything to say. Then, in an attempt to fill the sudden silence, she blurted out, "I wore jeans. I hope that's okay." *Oh, God, you're an idiot! What a stupid thing to say. He's not blind. He can see you're wearing jeans.*

"Of course it's okay. I only wish I'd had the foresight to bring in some comfortable clothes this morning. From now on, I will." So saying, he took off his tie and unbuttoned the top button of his pale blue shirt. "You hungry yet? Or do you want to work for a while, then eat later?"

"Let's work for a while and eat later."

For the next hour, they discussed the first commercial and whether the agency should gamble and actually shoot it or whether they should demonstrate the concept on storyboards.

"Presenting Rousseau with an actual commercial would be more effective, wouldn't it?" Jenny said.

"Yes, except if he's not crazy about the actors we use, we might actually undermine our efforts. Sometimes, imagination is a more powerful tool when trying to sell something."

The thought crossed Jenny's mind that she'd heard the same thought expressed in terms of the explicitness of TV and movie scenes where the actors made love.

"Besides," Simon said, "in order to do a first-rate job on the commercial, we'd have to spend a lot of money. Maybe more money than we're willing to gamble."

"Really? I would have thought it could be done fairly inexpensively."

Simon smiled. "You're thinking in terms of home videos. I'm thinking in terms of renting a studio, hiring a director, an editor, actors, top-notch cameramen . . . it would cost a small fortune."

He named a figure that took Jenny's breath away.

"I had no idea," she said.

"Actually, video storyboards will be almost as effective as real people on film," Simon said.

"Explain what a video storyboard is." Jenny vaguely remembered Simon using the term in conversation, but she'd never paid close attention.

"Well, rather than a static series of vignettes, the artist renders the concept, and the drawings are filmed individually—similar to the way animated films are made. Then a voice-over and music are added," Simon explained.

Once the decision was made to use video storyboards, they began to write a script for the first commercial.

Jenny suggested they work directly on the computer. "It'll be faster," she said.

"You don't know how slow I type," Simon said.

"Well, I type fast. Besides, I do my best composing sitting at the computer."

"Okay. You're the boss." Simon pulled a chair up next to Jenny, and the whole time they worked, she could feel him only inches away. She could smell faint traces of the cologne he'd put on that morning, and when he leaned in to see the screen, she could feel the warmth of his body, and her pulse would quicken.

Even when she wasn't looking directly at him, she could feel him there—so close—close enough to touch. Once, as he leaned over her, she felt his breath on the back of her neck. Her heart thumped so hard, she was afraid he'd hear it, and her fingers fumbled on the keys.

She had to force herself to concentrate on the work, but it was hard. She kept thinking that all she had to do was turn, move her head, and they would be close enough to kiss again.

What would he do if she did move? Would he kiss her? Or was he sorry about last night? Did he wish it had never happened?

Quit thinking about last night!

About seven forty-five, Simon said, "I'm hungry."

Jenny sat back and stretched, her T-shirt tightening over her breasts. "Me, too." Still stretching, she looked at Simon, and when she did, she caught him staring at her chest with a funny expression on his face. Suddenly self-conscious, Jenny hurriedly dropped her arms.

"What do you feel like eating?" he said, standing, avoiding eye contact.

Jenny's face felt warm, but she managed a casual shrug. "I don't care." She pushed her chair out so she could get up, and he carefully moved out of her way.

"There's a good hamburger place over on Richmond, and they deliver," he said, still not looking directly at her.

"That sounds good." He'd been looking at her *breasts!*

Simon called in their order, and while they waited for their food, they reviewed what they'd already written, and Jenny tried to stop thinking about the funny look on Simon's face and the way he'd been staring at her breasts, but the thoughts were there. She tried to remember if anything like that had ever happened before, and she couldn't recall a single incident. Her seedling of hope grew a little stronger.

Within thirty minutes, their food was delivered. Jenny noticed that Simon put the width of the desk between them, settling himself across from her.

While they ate, Jenny told him about Bob Hennessey and their meeting that morning.

"So what's he like?" Simon said around a mouthful of his cheeseburger.

"Way too good-looking."

Simon frowned. "Too good-looking?"

"You know, one of those too-good-to-be-true guys who looks like he belongs in the pages of *Gentlemen's Quarterly.*" Jenny laughed. "You should see him. He's got thick blond hair, a deep tan, and the most unbelievable blue-green eyes. He's got to be wearing colored contact lenses. No one has eyes that incredible."

Simon's frown deepened. "I didn't know you were so impressed by good looks."

Jenny started to say not to be ridiculous, she wasn't, and then she stopped. Why, Simon almost sounded as if he was jealous. The thought excited her even more than catching him staring at her breasts. Maybe Becky had been on to something.

"Guess I had you fooled," she said, purposely coy. She kept expecting him to laugh, to realize she was pulling his leg, but he didn't.

"Is this guy married?" Simon said, face stiff.

Jenny smothered a smile. "I don't think so." She mentally crossed her fingers. "He certainly doesn't act like he's married." It was just a tiny white lie, but she felt guilty all the same.

"You'd better be careful, Jenny," Simon said darkly. "This Hennessey sounds like a slick customer."

"Don't worry about me," she said. "I know how to take care of myself."

"That's what Marie Antoinette said."

Jenny laughed. She couldn't help it. "Oh, for heaven's sake, Simon. I'm not the least bit interested in Bob Hennessey, and even if I were, I could certainly handle him. I'm not stupid, you know."

For the rest of the evening, she kept thinking about how Simon had reacted to her description of Bob Hennessey. That, added to what had happened earlier when she'd stretched and he'd stared, made her heart feel lighter than it had for a long time.

Because if Simon was jealous—and he'd certainly *acted* as if he was—that meant he had feelings for her.

Feelings that had nothing to do with friendship.

Now all she had to figure out was how she was going to get him to admit it.

Chapter Seven

Philippe Rousseau loved the idea. "It's wonderful," he told Simon. "Everything I had hoped for, and more. Truly inspired. You and Mark are to be congratulated."

Simon expelled a quiet sigh of relief. He hadn't really been worried, but there was always the possibility that a client wouldn't like a proposed campaign, no matter how brilliant the ad agency thought the presentation was.

"Great," he said. "That means we can get started casting the lead actor and actress, then. I've been through the list of possible candidates and have come up with several I think could work well." He reached for a thick portfolio.

An hour later, Rousseau leaned back in his chair

and sighed. "I'm sorry, Simon. I haven't seen anyone I would want to play the parts of Zach and Mallory."

Simon nodded wearily. He had already come to the same conclusion. Rousseau had been shown the complete roster of available people. Short of putting out a general casting call and looking at unknowns, they had exhausted all known possibilities. "This complicates matters."

"Nevertheless, I am not willing to compromise. I know what I want, and this campaign is too important to settle for less."

"What is it you're looking for that you haven't found?" Simon asked patiently. It wouldn't do to let Rousseau see his frustration.

"Fresher faces," Rousseau said without hesitation. "People who haven't been seen before. People who look real, like someone you would pass on the street. Most of these actors and actresses you've shown me look like models. They are too perfect. And the ones who aren't too perfect are too recognizable. Even I, who do not know much about your business, recognize some of the faces." His dark eyes glowed with intensity. "When those commercials are shown, I want every parent to see their own children when they see Zach and Mallory. I want every young woman to see herself, every young man to see himself."

Simon nodded. "I'll keep looking."

Rousseau studied Simon thoughtfully for a long moment. "You know," he said slowly, "you would be ideal for the role of Zach."

"Me?" Simon said. "But I'm not an actor—" He stopped, chuckling. "Unless of course you count the time I played the part of a tomato in my third-grade play. And believe me, I was less than a rousing success, especially when I tripped over my own feet and squashed my costume." Simon would never forget the chagrin on his mother's face at his ignominious fall. Leona Christopher was not accustomed to anything less than perfection.

Rousseau smiled, but his eyes remained contemplative. "Yes, you are exactly the type of young man I envisioned when you showed me your concept."

The idea of playing Zach in the commercial was unexpectedly appealing. Simon had been bored stiff for months. The challenge of designing this campaign was all that had saved him. And once this campaign was well under way, and the commercials were actually being filmed, he would probably be bored again.

He looked at Rousseau. "Are you serious about me?"

Rousseau smiled. "Yes, I think I am."

Simon returned his smile. Playing the role of Zach would be fun. "You might change your mind when you see me on film."

"Perhaps."

Just then, Simon's intercom buzzed, and Cherry said, "Simon, Miss Randall is here."

"Oh, good." Even though all of their recent time together had been tinged with awkwardness, Simon smiled. Today was Jenny's day off, and he'd asked her to come by to meet Rousseau. "Tell her I'll be right out," he told the receptionist.

"This is the friend I mentioned," he said to Rousseau, "the one who came up with the idea for the campaign. She's also written much of the copy for the first three commercials. I thought you would enjoy meeting her, so I asked her to stop by today.''

"Of course.''

The two men headed down the hall to the reception area, a starkly modern room with chrome-and-steel furniture, pale gray carpeting and burgundy leather couches. Glass outer walls overlooked the twentieth-floor elevator banks.

Jenny rose from her seat. She smoothed down the skirt of her blue dress before walking toward them.

She looked awfully pretty today, Simon thought. He smiled at her. "Hi, Jenny. Glad you could make it.''

"Hi.'' Her dark eyes were bright with curiosity as they moved from Simon to Philippe Rousseau.

"Jenny, this is Philippe Rousseau, the owner of Hill Country Wines. Philippe, this is Jenny Randall.''

"It's such a pleasure to meet you, Mr. Rousseau.'' Smiling, Jenny extended her hand.

Simon kept looking at her, wondering what was different. Then he realized she'd fixed her hair in a new way. It was fluffier, or something. And she was wearing earrings. Jenny never wore earrings.

"The pleasure is all mine,'' Rousseau said. "And please, Mr. Rousseau sounds so formal and makes one feel quite old. I would be honored if you would call me Philippe.''

To Simon's amazement, Rousseau took her hand, but instead of shaking it as any normal man would do, he raised it to his lips and kissed it. He also held on to it for an inordinately long time—so long that Simon felt like yanking it away from him.

A becoming pink stained Jenny's cheeks, and her dark eyes shone with pleasure. "Philippe,'' she said softly. She seemed mesmerized by Rousseau, who continued to smile at her.

Why was it that all women seemed to love that hand-kissing stuff? Simon thought in disgust.

"Simon tells me you're the one responsible for the brilliant idea for my advertising campaign," Rousseau said.

"Oh, you like it, then?" Her smile expanded in delight.

"I am convinced it will put Hill Country Wines on every shopping list."

"I'm so glad. I know Alonzo and Christopher will do a great job."

"I have every confidence in them."

Jenny looked at Simon, her eyes filled with triumph. He knew she felt the same elation he did over winning the account. If they'd been alone, they'd probably have let out a few war whoops.

"Well," she said, "I guess I'd better be going. I know you're probably busy, and I have errands to run."

"Oh, but you're not leaving so soon," Rousseau protested before Simon could answer. "I was just about to suggest that we break for lunch. Won't you join us? It would be my great honor to have both of you as my guests."

"Oh, well, I hadn't planned on taking the time for lunch." Jenny turned a questioning gaze to Simon.

Simon didn't like the way Rousseau was looking at Jenny. But he didn't see how he could refuse the invitation or discourage her from coming along. "Oh, come on, Jenny. You have to eat lunch."

Jenny smiled and turned to Rousseau. "Well, if you're sure I wouldn't be in the way. . ."

"In the way?" Rousseau said. "How could a beautiful, charming young woman possibly be in the way?"

Jenny's eyes sparkled. "When you put it that way, how can I refuse?"

"Good. That's settled then. Shall we go?" With a flourish, Rousseau presented her with his arm.

Laughing up at him, she took it. Neither looked at Simon.

Simon nearly gagged. He wondered what had ever possessed him to suggest Jenny come to the office to meet Rousseau. It was like leading a lamb to slaughter. She was entirely too inexperienced. He should never have exposed her to someone as smooth and experienced as Philippe Rousseau.

Because Simon's Corvette couldn't seat three, they rode in Rousseau's Mercedes. He took them to Brennan's, which was ordinarily one of Simon's favorite restaurants.

"This is a real treat," Jenny said. "I usually just have a sandwich or something quick for lunch."

"You Americans are always in such a hurry," Rousseau said. "Food is meant to be savored. Eaten slowly, accompanied by a glass of wine...and a lovely companion." Rousseau smiled warmly at her as they waited to be seated.

Jenny flushed with pleasure.

How had Simon gotten himself into this? Was he going to have to sit and listen to Rousseau slather on the charm throughout their meal?

And Jenny. Usually she was so astute about people. Didn't she realize Rousseau was a practiced con artist when it came to women?

Twenty minutes later, Simon knew his fears were going to be realized, only it was worse than he'd imagined. Rousseau no longer seemed to be acting. In fact, he seemed totally beguiled by Jenny, and she had certainly fallen under his spell.

Simon might as well not even have been there, for all the attention the two of them paid to him.

"So you're the editor of a newspaper?" Rousseau said. They had just been served their turtle soup, a specialty of the house. "That must be a fascinating occupation."

Jenny waited while their waiter poured a dollop of sherry into her soup. "Sometimes it is. At other times it's just as boring as any other job." She picked up her spoon. "You're the one with the fascinating work."

"Yes, I must admit wine making is never boring. Each day brings a new challenge."

"You're lucky."

"When things are going well, I consider myself lucky. At other times, especially when the weather doesn't cooperate, I wonder why I didn't pick an easier way to make a living." He broke off a piece of a hard roll. "Do you know anything about wine making?"

"No. Not much," she admitted.

"Jenny has a green thumb," Simon interjected. He was tired of being ignored. "I told her she'd really enjoy seeing your vineyards."

Rousseau frowned. "What is this *green thumb?* I don't believe I know the term."

Jenny laughed. "It means I like to grow things."

"Ah," Rousseau said. "Then, yes, if you love to grow things, you would love my vineyards. You should come and tour the winery some weekend."

Simon could have kicked himself for bringing up the subject of Jenny's interest in growing things, even though, before today, he had thought about taking Jenny to Hill Country Winery himself. Now, however, he realized the best thing he could do for Jenny was to keep her far away from Philippe Rousseau and his slick line.

"Simon offered to take me sometime," Jenny said. Her gaze turned to Simon.

He knew he should smile and say something nice, but he didn't feel like it.

"Good," Rousseau said. "I will look forward to your visit. Plan to stay overnight, and I will give a small dinner party for you."

"Oh, you don't have to go to any trouble—"

"Trouble? How could it be trouble to have a dinner party with good food and good wine and good friends? *Au contraire,* I would enjoy it very much. Let's settle on a time for you to come before I leave for home."

"When *are* you leaving?" Simon asked.

"I had planned to leave this afternoon if our business was concluded, but since we haven't yet settled on an actress to play the part of Mallory, perhaps I should stay until we do." He laid his soup spoon in his empty bowl. "That was excellent turtle soup."

"Yes, it *is* wonderful," Jenny agreed, finishing her last spoonful. Then, looking at Simon, she added,

"Does that mean you have chosen someone to play Zach?"

Simon laughed a bit self-consciously. "Well, believe it or not, Philippe has suggested I play the part of Zach."

Jenny's eyes widened. "Really?" She seemed taken aback, but slowly, a delighted smile spread across her face. "That's a great idea. You're perfect for the role."

"Yes, that is what I thought," Rousseau said.

Just then, their waiter came to clear off their soup bowls and serve their main course. When the man left, Rousseau said, "We've talked long enough about me and the winery and the campaign. I want to hear about you, Jenny. Tell me about your husband."

"Oh . . . I'm not married."

"But you have a—what's that awkward term you Americans use—a *significant other?*"

Jenny laughed softly. "No, I don't. I'm completely unattached."

Rousseau made an exaggerated gesture of disbelief. "I will never understand Americans. What is wrong with the men in this country if they've allowed such an enchanting young woman to remain single?" His dark eyes rested on Jenny's face. "They must all be blind."

Simon felt nauseated. Rousseau's practiced flattery and Jenny's obvious enjoyment of it was all too much.

It was going to be a long lunch.

Jenny was having a wonderful time.

Philippe Rousseau was handsome, charming and flatteringly attentive.

Oh, she knew he would have been flatteringly attentive even if she'd had crossed eyes and a wart on her nose, but that didn't stop her from enjoying herself.

What woman wouldn't?

Besides, maybe Philippe's attentions would make Simon jealous. Jenny mentally crossed her fingers and hoped her gaze was adoring enough as she looked at Philippe.

He really *was* devastatingly attractive. He wasn't extremely tall, perhaps about five feet ten, but he was well built, with an interesting, angled face and dark, glowing eyes that looked at a woman as if she were the only woman in the room. And that lovely French accent, that quaint, slightly formal way of speaking. She loved it all.

Jenny wondered how old he was. She guessed somewhere in his middle to late forties. Fifty, tops. Why was it that as men aged, they just seemed to get more attractive?

During their meal, Philippe asked her about her family. "I have three older sisters," she said. "They're all married and among them they have seven children."

"And your parents? Are they still living?"

Jenny smiled. "Oh, yes. Dad's retired, and Mom works as a school secretary." She laughed. "My mother says she's never going to retire because she would go crazy if she had to stay home all day with my father."

"Yes, I understand," Philippe said. "Too much, how do you say it? *Togetherness?* It takes all the mystery out of a relationship." His voice lowered intimately. "There must always be mystery between a man and a woman, is that not right?"

"Oh, absolutely," Jenny said. She glanced at Simon. He had been awfully quiet for a long time. His gaze met hers, and he frowned.

A delicious thrill raced through her. He was definitely not happy. She turned back to Philippe. "What about you, Philippe? Are you married?"

He shook his head sadly. "I am a widower."

"Oh, I'm sorry," Jenny said.

He shrugged. "It's been a long time. Dominique died more than ten years ago, when our daughter was only five."

"Oh, so you have a teenage daughter?"

"Yes, Giselle is fifteen. And becoming more and more impossible every day." But he said it with love and pride, and Jenny knew he adored his daughter. She liked him all the more.

By now they were finished with their meal.

Their waiter asked if they wanted dessert.

"I don't think so," Simon said. He looked at his watch. "It's getting late. I know Jenny has things to do and we—"

"Nonsense," Philippe interjected. "No meal is complete without dessert. And I was told that they have a wonderful crème brûlé here."

"Oh," Jenny said, "the crème brûlé is to die for." It was her very favorite dessert.

"We must have it, then," Philippe said.

Jenny looked at Simon.

Simon glowered.

Jenny was almost afraid to hope that Simon's obvious displeasure stemmed from jealousy, yet what else could it be?

When their dessert was served, Jenny almost hated to take a bite, it looked so beautiful. Brennan's served the dessert garnished with fresh raspberries, strawberries and blueberries. Jenny carefully spooned a dark raspberry and some of the burnt sugar and cream into her spoon. She closed her eyes as she savored the almost heavenly taste. "Mmm, wonderful," she said on a sigh.

Rousseau smiled indulgently and started to take a bite of his own, then suddenly put down his spoon and stared at Jenny. "Mallory."

Jenny blinked. "Pardon me?"

"Mallory!" Rousseau exclaimed. "My God, Jenny, talk about being blind. I've been looking at you for more than an hour, and it just occurred to me. You are perfect for the role of Mallory in our commercials. When you sighed like that and said 'Mmm, wonderful,' I could just see you savoring Hill Country champagne or Chardonnay with that exact expression on your face."

Jenny was so stunned, she couldn't think of a thing to say.

Rousseau turned to Simon. "Do you see what I mean?"

Simon stared at Rousseau. He was obviously too surprised to answer, either.

Rousseau beamed, his gaze moving from one to the other. "You two are exactly the kind of people I envisioned when you presented the idea for the ongoing story. You, Simon, as Zach." His gaze turned back to Jenny. "And you, my lovely Jenny, as Mallory." His voice rang with conviction. "That's it! You two are the perfect combination."

Chapter Eight

Jenny stared at Philippe.

She couldn't believe she'd heard him correctly. "B-but I'm not an actress," she finally sputtered.

"I don't want an actress for the role of Mallory. I want you," Rousseau insisted. His dark eyes gleamed with fervor.

"But I already have a job." Jenny looked at Simon. Wasn't he going to say something?

Simon met her gaze reflectively. "You know...that's not a bad idea."

"Simon! I can't do this!" Jenny shook her head in disbelief. "You two are crazy."

"Why can't you do it?" Philippe asked.

"I told you why not. I'm not an actress, and I already have a job."

"But you told me yourself you're worried about what might happen at the paper.... Doing this would give you some extra money, just in case," Simon said.

He had a point, Jenny thought.

"Why are you worried about your job?" Philippe asked, frowning.

"I'm not exactly worried. Maybe *concerned* is a better word." Jenny hesitated, then sighed. She hurriedly explained her situation to Philippe, ending with, "But that doesn't mean I'm going to leave the paper. I haven't made any decisions yet. I'm waiting to see what happens first. I may be concerned for nothing." She looked at Simon again. Surely he could see this idea was too farfetched to consider seriously.

"Would you agree to at least test for the part of Mallory?" Philippe suggested. "To see if you can do it?"

"But—"

"Yes, Jenny, why not test?" Simon urged.

"I just don't think..." Jenny trailed off. Why had Simon so readily agreed with Philippe? Couldn't he see that the whole idea was ridiculous? She turned to Philippe. "Why do you want me, anyway?"

Philippe smiled. "That's easy. You have just the freshness, just the wholesome, girl-next-door look that I think is perfect."

"But even if I agreed, when would we work? I'm committed to the paper four out of seven days," Jenny argued.

"We could shoot on Tuesdays, when you're off," Simon said, "and evenings and weekends." He looked at Rousseau. "It might cost more money if we shoot at odd times, you know."

"How much more?"

"I don't know. Depends on who we use. But on the other hand, shooting at night would leave the studio free for other clients during the day." Simon shrugged. "If we use a new production company...one eager to build a steady clientele, this might even work to your advantage."

"I will have to talk to my investors, of course," Rousseau said, "but I don't foresee any problems. They've committed their full support to this effort."

He turned to Jenny again. "Please, Jenny, think about this. The work would take only about three months—isn't that right, Simon?—and I will make it worth your while financially. For the series of ten commercials, I would be willing to pay you twenty-five thousand dollars."

She took a deep breath. That much. Almost an entire year's salary at the paper. For approximately three months' work.

She couldn't help thinking how a sum of money like that would provide a nest egg in case she decided to quit her job. And having a nest egg would give her options. Choices. She would not be at someone else's mercy. She would be master of her own fate.

But acting in a commercial?

Wasn't she the one who had constantly accused Simon of selling out?

She thought hard.

Would she be selling out?

No. Doing these commercials would not be selling out.

Doing these commercials would be a one-time shot, a means to an end.

Plus—her heart skipped at the thought—there was the added, nearly irresistible incentive of working with Simon. Pretending to be married to Simon.

Images flashed through Jenny's mind. They would be young lovers. They would have to kiss each other. Caress each other.

Jenny's breathing quickened.

For weeks on end, they would be portraying a newly married, romantic couple.

She swallowed.

Something twisted in her stomach and her heart thumped harder as she envisioned all the days, all the nights, all the delicious and wonderful scenes they would play.

Here was her opportunity.

Opportunity only knocks once, her mother's voice whispered in Jenny's head.

A shimmering excitement raced through her veins.

"I'll do it," she heard herself say.

"You're what?" Becky said.

Her incredulous question was followed by a babble of excited voices.

It was the Sunday afternoon following Jenny's lunch with Philippe and Simon, and she had just broken the news about her new venture to her family.

"I can't believe it," Jenny's mother said. "Why, that's so *exciting!*" Lois Randall's dark eyes, which both Becky and Jenny had inherited, sparkled with interest. "And you say these commercials will be shown all over the country?"

"Yes," Jenny said.

"Gosh," Cindy said, "I think I'm jealous."

In her former life, sans husband and kids, Cindy had dreamed of becoming a model, and Jenny had always thought her sister was certainly pretty enough to have accomplished her goal.

Yet here was Jenny, the kid sister, the one with the brains and athletic ability, doing what Cindy, the one with all the beauty, would have given anything to do.

"Are you quitting your job at the *Vanguard?*" Kate asked. At forty-four, Kate was the oldest and the most practical of the sisters.

"No way," Jenny said. "It's not like acting is going to be my life's work. This is a one-time shot. Just to give me a nest egg."

"Aren't you nervous?" Becky asked. "I mean, you've never done anything like this before. What if you're no good at it?"

"They're testing me on Tuesday. If I'm no good, they'll have to find someone else, that's all. I'm not worried about it." Jenny shrugged, although she didn't feel as casual about the outcome as she was pretending.

In the five days since she'd made the decision to accept Philippe's offer, she had gone from an initial reluctance and disbelief to a passionate desire to play Mallory.

She hadn't decided if her total change of heart was due to the money that would give her such an edge or the almost unbearable excitement that had been generated by the thought of the intimacy with Simon.

She knew that if she flubbed the test, she would be horribly disappointed.

I won't flub. I won't flub.

This was her new mantra, and she'd said it dozens of times during the past couple of days.

"How much money are they going to pay you?" her mother asked.

Jenny couldn't help smiling. Although her mother would never dream of asking her sons-in-law how much money they made, she thought nothing of quizzing her daughters about such matters.

Jenny told her. "Plus, they've said I can keep my wardrobe from the shoot."

Her mother's mouth made an astonished "Oh."

"Yes, that's how I felt," Jenny said. "I couldn't have turned down this job. Not when that money will be my cushion if things go downhill at the paper." Under her breath she muttered, "As I'm very much afraid they might."

"What's wrong, Punkin?" her dad said, using his pet name for her. His hazel eyes reflected concern. "You having trouble with the new manager?"

Jenny grimaced. "No, not yet, but...I don't know. I don't have a good feeling about him."

Her dad wanted to be updated on everything that had happened at work. For the next half hour, Jenny gave him a complete rundown. Then it was time for dinner. While they ate, the conversation turned back to the commercial.

"Do you think I could come and watch when you're filming?" Cindy asked.

"I don't know." Jenny didn't want her sister there. She didn't want anyone from her family there. It was going to be tricky enough to act as Simon's fiancée and then his wife without giving her emotions away, let alone having to do it in front of family.

"Would you ask? I'd love to come."

"I'll see," Jenny promised. She crossed her fingers in her lap. She wasn't really fibbing, so why did she feel bad?

Later that afternoon, after they'd had dinner and cleaned up the kitchen, Becky drew Jenny aside. Her eyes were shining. "Jen," she whispered, "do you realize that this might be your chance with Simon?"

Jenny didn't pretend to misunderstand. "I know." Just thinking about it, Jenny could feel the butterflies starting up in her stomach again.

Becky squeezed her hand. "Good luck, sweetie. Keep me posted, okay?"

"I will."

"Call me Tuesday and let me know how the test went."

"All right."

Jenny sent up a silent prayer.

This just had to work out.

It simply had to.

Within a week, Simon had lined up a studio. They were using a newly formed production company with a brand-new studio out in Katy, a town just west of Houston.

If all went well, and they didn't have to scurry around to find new leads, they would start shooting the first commercial during the coming weekend and finish up any retakes on the following Tuesday.

Although normally a thirty-second spot that was shot on-site at a studio would only take a day, maybe two, Simon wanted to be prepared for any contingencies. Philippe Rousseau and his investors were sinking an astronomical amount of money into this advertising campaign, and everything had to be perfect. It was a huge risk for them, and Simon felt privileged and excited about being a part of it.

He and Tom Ridgeway, his art director, spent long hours in conference with the producer and his assistant, the set designer and the rest of the creative team.

Because Simon was so busy, he hadn't seen much of Jenny. Today, however, was the day of her test. Funny how they were all thinking of it as Jenny's test, when in reality, he was being tested, too.

Who knew? He might be terrible, and Rousseau might decide he wanted someone else to play the part of Zach. Wouldn't that be ironic? If Jenny, who had been so reluctant to even test, did well and ended up playing Mallory, and Simon, who hadn't balked at all, ended up being replaced?

Simon looked at his watch. Rousseau was driving in from the winery this morning and should arrive at any time. Jenny was also due at the studio in ten minutes. They would shoot the test in approximately two hours after a wardrobe and makeup session.

Simon walked over to look at the set again. Originally, when he and Jenny had first talked about the idea, the first commercial was conceived as being a two-parter. He'd envisioned it filmed with two different interiors—the first at the wine shop, the second at Mallory's apartment. Since then, they'd decided that concept was too expensive. The thirty-second spot would work better, cost less, and be more practical to produce if it had only one background—Mallory's apartment.

The set designer had done a good job, Simon thought. The set looked like a typical young working woman's living room and was furnished with contemporary, inexpensive furniture, bright pillows and framed prints on the walls.

The scene would open with the cameras focused on Jenny, who would be sitting on her couch with a magazine on her lap. She would idly turn the page, then her doorbell would ring, and she would smile and jump up, hurry to the door, and fling it wide.

Simon, playing Zach, would be standing in the doorway, a bottle of Hill Country Wine cradled in one arm and a bouquet of pink baby roses in the other.

The two of them would greet each other, Jenny would lift her face and Simon would kiss her lightly. They would be laughing, and he would hand her the roses.

She would look inquiringly at the wine, and when she saw the label, her eyes would widen and she would ask what the occasion was.

The scene would progress from there: pouring the wine, the two of them drinking the wine, him getting down on one knee and proposing, her saying yes and then the two of them in a passionate embrace while a voice-over said, "Hill Country Wine—the only choice for the special occasions in your life...."

Simon stared pensively at the set as he thought about the upcoming test.

That passionate-embrace part at the end was what was bothering him.

It had been bothering him every time he thought about it.

He kept remembering the unexpected burst of desire he'd felt the night he twirled Jenny around the kitchen, then kissed her.

And how he'd promised himself he wouldn't do anything like that again. Not if he wanted to keep their friendship intact.

He knew he would have to be very, very careful during the filming.

He would have to make absolutely sure he kept his hormones, and his baser instincts, under control.

Jenny decided she loved being pampered. She loved having someone do her hair and someone else do her makeup. She loved being treated as if she were special.

She looked at herself in the mirror as Laine, the hairdresser, finished styling her hair. Jenny adored the new style. It was so sleek, so sophisticated and glamorous. Laine had cut Jenny's hair closer on the sides and nape and styled it fuller on the crown, which made Jenny look taller and so satisfyingly different than her normal breezy, casual cut had.

Becky had been right. Jenny had been wearing the same hairstyle since high school, and it *had* been time for a change.

Why hadn't she done something about her hair sooner?

And the makeup!

Jenny hadn't known makeup could look both natural and glamorous at the same time.

Suddenly she had cheekbones.

Jenny had always wanted cheekbones.

She just kept staring at herself. "I don't believe it," she finally said as Laine stood back to admire her handiwork. "I look almost beautiful."

"What's this 'almost' baloney?" Laine said. "You *are* beautiful."

When the wardrobe person, who introduced herself as Sally, zipped up the raspberry dress selected for the shoot, Jenny's breath caught.

She couldn't believe how the vibrant color flattered her. Why hadn't she been wearing colors like this all along? Suddenly she realized just how drab and washed out her normal beiges and light blues had made her look.

Even the way this dress was cut, snug through the bodice and over her waist, then gently flaring and ending a few inches above her knees, made her look different.

Sexy, she thought.

She looked sexy.

Excitement danced through her veins.

Would Simon be surprised when he saw her? She wondered what he would think.

Simon felt as if a bulldozer had run him over.

He couldn't believe this was Jenny.

She didn't look like herself at all. She looked...sexy. And provocative. Like someone completely different from the Jenny he'd always known.

And he didn't like it.

He didn't like it at all.

He scowled. Look how all the guys were fawning all over her. Dick Craig, the producer. And Tom Ridgeway, Simon's art director, who should know better.

The cameramen. The grips. Even the eighteen-year-old film student who Dick Craig had hired to be a gofer stood gawking with a stupid look on his face.

And Philippe Rousseau.

Hell, Rousseau was practically slobbering.

Ever since Jenny had come out of her dressing room, picking her way carefully around the cables and equipment littering the floor, every man in the place had been acting idiotic.

Except Simon, of course.

"Over here, Miss Randall," Dick Craig called now. He was standing next to the royal blue sofa where she would be sitting when the scene opened. His craggy face, incongruously topped by curly red hair, broke into a smile as she stepped into the light. "Yeah, that color's perfect for you," he said.

As instructed, she took her seat on the end of the royal blue couch. The lights were turned up, and Jenny blinked. The production assistant, a pretty blonde who didn't look a day over nineteen, arranged Jenny's dress so that it draped the way she wanted it to.

"Move a little more to the right," Craig said.

Hands poked and nudged her, arranged and rearranged her dress, her hair, the angle of her head.

Finally, everyone was satisfied. Dick Craig barked orders, and people scurried to fill them. He and Tom put their heads together, conferring quietly for a moment or two. Simon took his place behind the door. The production assistant handed him the wine and flowers. The hairdresser sprayed his hair one last time.

"Okay, everybody," Craig said. "Miss Randall? You ready?"

"Yes."

"Simon?"

"Yes."

"Action," Craig said.

Although Simon couldn't see her, he knew Jenny was turning the pages of her magazine and pretending to read. A few seconds later, the sound of the doorbell cut the silence. Simon took a deep breath, preparing himself.

Simon heard her footsteps, then the door was opened wide. She looked up, and their eyes met. Simon's breath caught.

Jenny smiled tremulously. "Hi, Zach," she said.

"Hi." He smiled and tried to still the unaccustomed skittering of his heart. Nerves, he thought. Just nerves.

Jenny lifted her face.

Simon's lips brushed hers. At the contact, the skittering became more pronounced. He told himself to calm down. This was no big deal. Just a test. No reason to be so nervous.

And then they were both moving into the room, and Jenny took the flowers from him, then looked at the bottle of wine and said, "Hill Country Wine! What's the occasion?" She sounded exactly the way Mallory should sound—excited and surprised.

Simon grinned and said, "You'll see." He felt calmer now, more sure of himself.

They moved through the rest of the scene. She put the flowers in a vase, he opened the wine, she brought out two champagne flutes, he poured the wine, they sat on the couch and drank some. Some of this action would end on the cutting-room floor, Simon knew.

Actually, a lot of it would. They would leave just enough for the viewer to know what had happened that they hadn't actually seen.

Then it was time for the proposal. Simon got down on one knee and took Jenny's hand. He looked into her eyes. They were so soft, so dark, so familiar. Something stirred deep inside him, and his voice was a little rough as he said his lines. "Mallory, I love you. Will you marry me?"

Jenny's eyes lit up, and her smile was tender and sweet and filled with happiness. "Yes, oh, yes," she said joyfully.

Simon got up and gently pulled her to a standing position. Then he enfolded her in his arms and kissed her. Jenny wound her arms around his neck and pressed herself close. Her mouth opened under his, and desire, sharp and sweet, zigzagged through him. Simon had to exercise every bit of self-control he possessed to keep his libido from running away with him.

God, she felt good in his arms.

"Cut," Dick Craig called.

Simon hurriedly released her, avoiding her eyes by turning toward the producer.

"That was great," Craig said, walking up to them on the set. "During the actual filming of the commercial, we'd want to do some things differently, but as a test, you both did a terrific job. Let's go see what it looks like on film."

In the screening room, as they watched the scene they'd filmed, Simon knew Craig was right. It was a superb test. If he hadn't known better, he'd have sworn he and Jenny were actually in love.

"For two people with no acting experience, you two certainly did a bang-up job," Craig said. "That's one of the best tests I've ever seen."

"It *was* wonderful. See, Jenny?" Philippe said. "I knew you would be excellent. You were worried for nothing."

Simon frowned. He was glad the test had gone well, of course he was. Then why did he have this feeling of foreboding?

Jenny hung around the studio, hoping that Simon would suggest they have dinner together that evening.

But he ignored her.

Finally, she had to admit defeat. He wasn't going to make any overtures in her direction. "Well," she said, "I guess I'll be going."

"Goodbye, Jenny," Philippe said, smiling warmly. "I'll see you next Tuesday." He took her hand and kissed it in farewell.

Jenny darted a look Simon's way, but he wasn't watching them. Disappointment flooded her. She'd thought…no, she *knew* he'd felt just as strongly about the kiss they'd shared today as she had. But he was obviously fighting those feelings. Why, she could only guess.

Resigned for now, she said goodbye to the rest of the crew, then purposefully walked up to Simon. "Bye, Simon. Guess I'll see you in the morning."

He turned. For a moment, their eyes met. Some emotion sparked in the depths of his, but whatever it was, he quickly extinguished it.

In fact, Jenny wasn't sure she hadn't imagined seeing something, when in reality, nothing had been there.

"Yes," he said offhandedly, giving her a quick smile. "See you at the track."

As she drove home, Jenny thought about the day and wondered what had been going through Simon's mind as they parted.

She sighed.

Simon's behavior was a downer, taking some of the edge off her elation at winning the role of Mallory.

But she wouldn't give up.

It would take more than Simon's reluctance to acknowledge the chemistry between them to discourage her.

She had loved him for a long time now. And no matter what it took for her to get him to admit he might have the same feelings for her, she would do it.

Chapter Nine

For the next six weeks, Jenny functioned in a perpetual state of nervous tension. The situation at work and the situation with Simon combined to keep her on tenterhooks.

At the paper, she felt as if she were constantly walking a tightrope, balancing precariously while waiting for Bob Hennessey to shake the rope and knock her off.

She wasn't alone.

The entire staff felt the tension, especially when Gloria left. On their boss's last day, Jenny and the rest of the staff gave Gloria a farewell party.

There were lots of tears shed—both by the employees and Gloria. There were lots of speeches, lots of reminiscing, lots of pathos and bathos.

Then suddenly she was gone, and it was just the staff and Hennessey.

Facing an unknown future.

Jenny watched the maneuvering as some of the staff members buttered him up. She might have been amused at the posturing and kowtowing if she hadn't been so anxious over what she was afraid would be the inevitable destruction of the paper as they knew it.

To her, it seemed obvious what Bob Hennessey would eventually do, despite his assurances that any proposals for changes would be carefully studied and implemented only if they would benefit the paper.

She had always loved the uncompromising standards of the *Vanguard*. When there was a problem in the community, the *Vanguard* wasn't afraid to tackle it. Gloria had believed—and the success of the paper had proven her right—that if the *Vanguard* was always fair and put the good of the community before the good of the bottom line, they would prosper, because the community would support them.

Jenny believed in this ideal wholeheartedly.

Unfortunately, she was afraid Hennessey didn't share those beliefs. The biggest problem was, Hennessey had no stake in the community, as Gloria and the rest of them did. He was only there temporarily.

Even if the new owner had not said so, it was obvious that someone like Bob Hennessey would not spend his future as the general manager of one small community paper.

No.

Hennessey was destined for much greater things in the Armstrong organization. He would stay in Houston just long enough to whip the *Vanguard* into whatever shape he and Armstrong envisioned for it, then he would be gone and someone else would take over the day-to-day management.

Jenny's greatest fear was that future decisions would be made strictly as to how they affected the bottom line. If that happened, if the *Vanguard's* principles were cast aside in favor of greater financial gain, Jenny could not remain as the editor.

Still, she wasn't quite ready to throw in the towel. So far, she had not butted heads with Hennessey. There had only been that one meeting between them, where he'd tiptoed around her. But each day, she waited. Any time now she expected him to tell her that he was changing the ratio of news to advertising from its current 40:60 to something like 30:70 or worse. If that happened, there was sure to be a decrease in the editorial staff. And that meant Jenny would lose either Thelma or Kim.

Waiting for the shoe to drop was getting to her.

And then there was Simon.

She sighed.

Being with Simon was no less stressful. Now there was an awkwardness between them that had not been there before. Because of it, Jenny could not truly relax in his company.

Yet, whether they were filming a commercial, running at the track or spending an evening together—which they did less and less often lately—she had to pretend everything was normal.

The pretending was getting to her.

In addition to the strain of feigning a normalcy that no longer existed, she was suffering a growing discouragement and disappointment.

Because no matter how much intimacy they shared when they were working on the commercials, it did not carry over into their private lives.

Just the opposite, in fact.

Simon had always been a toucher. In the years they had been friends, he was always draping his arm around her shoulders, hugging her, ruffling her hair, squeezing her hands, poking her good-naturedly.

But in the past few weeks, ever since that first kiss in her kitchen, he had barely touched her at all. And when they parted in the evenings, he gave her a chaste peck on the cheek and was very careful not to get too close.

Jenny hated this awkwardness between them.

Even filming the commercials was a bittersweet experience. Take yesterday, for instance.

Yesterday they had filmed the rehearsal dinner. Ten actors had been hired for the scene—three young women who were playing the parts of Mallory's bridesmaids, three young men who were the groomsmen and two older couples who were playing the parts of the parents of the engaged couple.

Jenny felt almost giddy as she walked onto the set. She was wearing the most provocative dress she'd ever owned—a gorgeous royal blue slip dress that clung to her figure, and Laine had given her a more dramatic hairstyle and makeup.

She felt by turns incredibly sexy and excruciatingly self-conscious as the soft material of her dress brushed against her skin. She could feel the gentle sway of the long, glittery earrings she wore, and when Kenny, the main cameraman, whistled at her, and Dick Craig winked, the most amazing and wonderful sense of elation and strength flooded her.

She looked out beyond the cameras and saw Philippe sitting just out of range. He smiled as their gazes met and put his fingers to his lips, kissing the tips and then opening his hands in a gesture that told her he thought she looked perfect.

Jenny lifted her head proudly, her self-consciousness ebbing away.

They all *liked* the way she looked!

As she stepped onto the set, she searched among the actors for Simon, expecting to see the same admiration on his face as evinced by the other men. But when she located him, standing behind the table where their "rehearsal dinner" would take place, her heart plummeted. His face looked stony, his eyes had a disapproving glint, almost an *angry* glint.

She stared at him for a moment, stunned. *He thinks I look ridiculous.* Unexpectedly, Jenny's temper rose. Where did he get off being so judgmental, anyway? What was wrong with him? Why was he acting this way? Everybody else liked the way she looked!

She lifted her chin defiantly and took her place next to him. "Hello," she said in her frostiest tone. She turned her attention to the table. She could feel his eyes on her, but she didn't look at him. Instead, she looked at the table.

The table looked beautiful, she thought, set with candles and flowers and pretty china. Each dinner plate was filled with what looked like half-eaten food.

Jenny knew that the first frame of this commercial would begin toward the end of the rehearsal dinner, so the producer wanted it to look as if the wedding party had already eaten most of the food.

As Dick Craig barked out his orders, and various assistants milled around, the actors took their places. Soon the filming began.

As rehearsed, the "guests" tapped their spoons against their champagne glasses. "Kiss, kiss, let's see a kiss!" they chanted, laughing and hooting. The actor playing Zach's best man prodded Simon in the back. "And no more pecks, either," he teased.

Simon grinned good-naturedly, saying, "Okay, okay," and then he reached for Jenny, pulling her up from her chair as he stood, himself. When his hands slid around her, Jenny felt their warmth through the thin material of her dress, and a shivery sensation raced over her body. She lifted her face.

Just before his lips met hers, their gazes connected, and Jenny saw that Simon's anger and disapproval— if that's what it had been—was gone. Now something else burned in the depths of his blue eyes, something fierce and elemental, something that caused her heart to knock against her rib cage.

And then he was kissing her, his mouth open and demanding, his tongue plunging into her mouth with an insistence that caused a hot lick of desire to arch through her body. She pressed against him, hardly hearing the continued hoots and catcalls as the "wedding party" cheered them on.

Her breasts tightened as Simon's hand splayed against the small of her back and urged her closer. It was then that she felt his arousal, and an answering heat pulsed deep inside her.

In that moment, they might have been the only two people in the universe. Everything else, everyone else, faded into the background, and there was only Simon. His mouth, his hands, his body and the way they were making her feel.

Simon was all that mattered.

Simon—and the love and need she felt for him.

The kiss seemed to last forever. Finally, they broke apart, Jenny's heart continuing its wild tattoo. For long seconds, she looked at him.

Lipstick was smeared on his mouth, and his eyes were filled with an unfamiliar gleam as they raked her. Jenny could feel her nipples pushing against the thin fabric of her dress, and she knew everyone else could probably see them, too. Briefly, embarrassment threatened her.

She tried to forget about herself, tried to remember that she was pretending to be Mallory, that Mallory would not be embarrassed by the evidence of her passion.

And then Jenny realized she wasn't embarrassed. In fact, she felt proud. She had made Simon feel desire for her. He *still* felt that desire. She could see the evidence of it in his eyes, in the way he was looking at her, and she knew the betraying physical evidence was probably still there, too.

She smiled slowly, thrilled by her knowledge and the feeling of power it evoked.

The script called for them to now pick up their wineglasses.

Simon picked up his.

She picked up hers.

As instructed, they intertwined their arms and drank from each other's glass, all the while maintaining eye contact.

Jenny knew that a voice-over would be added at this point, saying the familiar line about Hill Country Wine being perfect for all the viewers' special occasions.

Then, after the ceremonial wine tasting, Simon, still looking deep into her eyes, said his rehearsed line, "I love you."

Jenny's head knew the words were part of the script, but her heart had no such knowledge. Trembling, she whispered her answer, "I love you, too."

Dick Craig called, "That's a wrap!" and noise erupted around them.

Craig walked toward the set. "Great acting, you guys."

Jenny wanted to look at Simon, but she didn't quite dare. She hadn't been acting, and she didn't think he'd been, either. She wondered if he would say something to her. But then people started moving around, and Simon's art director approached him. Soon they were engaged in conversation, Simon's back turned to her. A moment later, Philippe walked up to Jenny and reached for her hands.

"Jenny, you were wonderful." He bent down to kiss her cheek.

Jenny smiled. "Thank you. I didn't know you would be here today."

He shrugged. "I hadn't planned to, but I couldn't seem to stay away." His eyes were warm as they rested on her face.

"I'm so glad you didn't," she said.

"Jenny, I wish I were staying in town tonight. I would love to take you to dinner."

"I would have enjoyed that."

Philippe smiled, then his gaze moved to her left, and Jenny knew Simon had turned around to join them.

"Good job today, Simon," Philippe said.

Jenny casually looked around. Her heartbeat accelerated.

"Thank you," Simon said stiffly. He avoided her eyes.

"Jenny, my dear," Philippe said, turning back to her, "I will see you this weekend. Perhaps we can have our dinner together then?" His smile was for her alone.

Feeling suddenly quite reckless, Jenny gave him her most dazzling smile and said, "I'll look forward to it."

Philippe raised her hands to his lips and kissed them in farewell, then turned to Simon and shook his hand. When he was gone, Jenny casually turned to Simon.

They hadn't spent an evening together in days. Maybe he would ask her to have dinner with *him* tonight. She knew he had heard what Philippe had said. She started to smile and say something innocuous.

"I think you'd better go get some clothes on," he said tightly.

The smile died on her lips. Her mouth dropped open.

"I also think you'd better be careful around that old lecher," he added. "Or you might get more than you're bargaining for!" And with that, he swung on his heel and walked away.

Jenny had just stood there, staring after him with her mouth open.

Remembering her outrage over his ridiculous and unfair remarks, she sighed. If only she could be sure they had been prompted by jealousy, she would be happy.

She stared at her computer screen. She'd been trying all morning to finish the editorial for this week's paper, without much success. She'd been unable to get yesterday off her mind.

If only she'd seen Simon this morning, been able to confront him and make some attempt to get their feelings out in the open, she would have felt better, but he hadn't shown up for their run.

She had a feeling he was avoiding her.

"Hey, Randall!"

Jenny looked up. Pete Cramer stood in her doorway, a big grin on his face.

"Oh, hi, Pete," she said.

"You want to grab a bite? Megan and I are going to Ninfa's for some quick Tex-Mex."

"Sure." Anything to take her mind off Simon.

Jenny hit F-10 to save, then opened her bottom desk drawer and extracted her purse. She smiled as she looked at it. It was new—a natural straw woven with raspberry and teal ribbons. She'd bought it to match the dress she'd worn during the filming of the first commercial, the dress she had on today. Getting to keep her wardrobe was one of the nicest perks of doing the commercials.

She slung the straps of the purse over her arm and walked out to meet Pete and Megan.

Pete gave a low whistle. "Wow," he said. "You look great. What are you doing to yourself?"

Pleasure warmed Jenny. "Thanks, Pete. It's just a new dress, that's all."

"It's more than a new dress," he said, giving her an appreciative once-over.

Pete's reaction was beginning to feel familiar. He wasn't the first male, or female, to compliment her on her appearance in the past weeks. Jenny knew she looked better than she ever had. She loved the fact that men were noticing her and flirting with her. It was a heady experience for someone who had always been treated like a kid sister. Yet, in some ways, her enjoyment of the attention she was receiving was an embarrassment.

Jenny had never thought of herself as a person who needed the admiration of men. She had scoffed at women who lived to please some man and had secretly felt superior to them.

So it was deflating to discover that she was just like every other woman on the face of the earth.

No matter what other accomplishments she had achieved, she still wanted to be considered attractive, sexy and desirable.

Especially by Simon.

Doing the commercials with Jenny had turned out to be sheer torment for Simon.

Holding her.

Kissing her.

It was driving him crazy.

She was driving him crazy.

He didn't know what was wrong with him. He couldn't seem to control the raw desire that grew stronger each time they were together.

He wished he'd never agreed to play the part of Zach. He definitely wished Jenny weren't playing the part of Mallory. Aside from the fact that she'd caused this terrible lust in him, he hated the way she was changing.

She was no longer the Jenny he knew.

He no longer felt comfortable with her.

He had liked her a hell of a lot better when she was just Jenny. Feisty and fun and easy to be with.

Doing these commercials had ruined everything between them, had made it impossible for him to just drop in on her as he had done for years. Now Simon was afraid to be around her. Afraid he might do or say something to give away his feelings.

Anytime they were together, all he could think about was the way she felt in his arms, the way she'd kissed him during the most recent commercial.

Simon swallowed and closed his eyes.

A vision of Jenny at the rehearsal dinner shoot filled his mind. That dress! Lord, that dress was enough to drive a man around the bend. The dress had clung to every curve, every hollow, defined every part of her body. When she walked, it had whispered over her skin, and Simon could feel himself losing control. He knew if he'd looked down, he would have seen a betraying bulge, and he was embarrassed and furious that she'd done this to him.

He'd glared at her. He'd alternately wanted to shake her for tempting him like that or rip the damned dress off of her and ravish her on the spot.

What in the hell was *wrong* with her? Why had she let them dress her like some kind of...*harlot?* Did she *like* having men undress her with their eyes? He'd never thought Jenny was like that.

And that Rousseau!

He had been present during the shooting of three of the five commercials they had under their belts. And the whole time, he'd practically drooled over Jenny. Geez, you would think a man of his age would know better. He was an old lecher, no doubt about it, and Simon wasn't sorry he'd told Jenny so. If she was too naive to realize what she was getting herself into, someone had to warn her.

Yeah, she definitely needed to be warned. The way she seemed to thrive on the attention she got from Rousseau and every other horny male on the set was disgusting.

Simon was disgusted with everything.

Nothing was turning out the way he'd envisioned.

He was dreading the commercial they planned to shoot this weekend—the wedding scene. Part of it would be shot at a beautiful old cathedral downtown—a perfect location with lots of stained glass and dark woods. The last part would be shot at a local country club, where the "reception" was being held.

And Rousseau would be there again, and Simon would have to endure yet another weekend of watching him slobber all over Jenny.

Simon picked up a pencil from his desk.

And Rousseau had invited her to have dinner with him!

Simon snapped the pencil in two.

Dinner. Ha! It wasn't dinner Rousseau was interested in. He was interested in getting her in the sack. All you had to do was look at him to know that.

Simon couldn't wait for the commercials to be completed.

He wanted his life to go back to the way it had been before. He wanted his relationship with Jenny to go back to what it had been before. He wanted Jenny to go back to being the Jenny she'd been before.

But he was sorely afraid none of that would ever happen.

Jenny rubbed her forehead wearily. It was late Friday afternoon, and she was tired and wanted to go home. Last night, they'd rehearsed for the commercial they would shoot this weekend, and it had been a terrible strain. Simon had been cold and distant, and when he did speak to her, he had been sarcastic. She'd been on the verge of tears more than once. Added to that, she hadn't gotten to bed until after midnight. And today had been an unusually busy day at the paper.

Unfortunately, she couldn't go home yet. She was waiting for a phone call from an important source she'd interviewed for her lead story.

She looked at her watch. Ten after five. He was supposed to have called her by four-thirty.

Finally, her call came through. She talked to her source, then hurriedly typed up her notes and turned off her computer. By the time she was ready to leave, it was almost six.

Just as she was gathering up her things, there was a knock on her office door. A second later, Bob Hennessey walked in. "Good. I caught you before you left," he said, giving her one of his toothpaste smiles.

Jenny groaned inwardly. She wasn't in the mood for Bob Hennessey tonight. "I was just leaving," she said firmly.

"No problem. Listen, I need you to sit in for me at a benefit luncheon tomorrow."

"I'm sorry, Bob. I can't."

"Why not?"

"Because I have a prior commitment."

His smile never slipped. "Well, you'll just have to break it. This luncheon is very important."

Jenny counted to five. She would not get upset. "My commitment is very important, too. It's also unbreakable." She reached down into her bottom drawer and retrieved her purse. "Tell you what. I'll call Thelma, see if she can go." Thelma was the assistant editor.

"I don't think you understand," Hennessey said smoothly. "I want *you.* This is a big deal. There will be a lot of important people there. Lots of prospective advertisers. I think, at the very least, if they can't have the general manager, they will expect the senior editor to attend as my emissary."

"And if I didn't already have this prior commitment, I would be happy to go," Jenny said patiently. She was determined to stay calm and reasonable. "But I do, so I can't."

Hennessey's eyes narrowed. "Just what *is* this unbreakable commitment?"

Jenny stared at him. It was none of his business what she was doing tomorrow. She knew it, and he knew it. Still, for some perverse reason, she decided she would tell him. "Tomorrow I am filming the sixth in a series of ten commercials."

He frowned. "Filming?"

"Yes. Filming. I'm playing one of the lead roles."

"Acting, you mean?"

"Yes, acting."

"Are you an aspiring actress, then?" He seemed amused by the idea.

"No." Just what did he find so amusing? "This is a one-time role. I have no desire to build a career as an actress. I'm simply doing this for the extra money," she added, then almost kicked herself. Now, why had she said that?

His eyes turned cold. "The position of editor is not a nine-to-five job. I thought you understood that."

"I don't remember anything in my job description that says I have to attend luncheons on Saturdays," Jenny countered. Her heart sped up. Even though her job was very important to her, and she was still hoping this new ownership would work out, she refused to compromise her principles. "Besides, you don't pay me enough money to demand twenty-four-hour-a-day availability." *Put that in your pipe and smoke it!* she thought angrily.

Only the faint flush of color on his neck and the glacial glint in his eyes betrayed his feelings. His voice was mild as he answered, "If we don't pay you enough money, perhaps you'd be happier somewhere else."

"Yes," Jenny said, looking him straight in the eyes. "Perhaps I would. Well, did you want me to call Thelma, or not?"

To her great satisfaction, his jaw tightened. "I'll call her myself."

"All right. See you Monday." Jenny gave him a cheery wave and walked out without a backward glance.

Simon waited at the front of the church. All of his anger was gone. Now he just felt jittery. Ruefully, he thought he couldn't be any more nervous if he were a real bridegroom waiting for his bride. He smoothed down the front of his gray morning coat and wondered what he was doing here.

All the cast members were in place.

Everything was ready.

Soon the bride would walk down the aisle to the strains of Mendelssohn.

After checking every detail one last time, Dick Craig called for action.

The organ music filled the church—rich, resonant sounds of celebration.

As instructed, Simon turned to look down the aisle. Although all of Jenny's walk toward the altar would not be used, Craig had explained that they would film all of it as well as the exchanging of the vows. Only a tiny segment would survive the final version—just enough to satisfy the viewers who would feel cheated if they didn't see part of the ceremony. At least two-thirds of the thirty-second spot would be reserved for the scene at the country club, because that's when Hill Country Wine would make its appearance.

One by one, the "bridesmaids" in their pink dresses did the hesitation step down the long aisle.

Simon took a deep breath.

The music swelled.

Sunlight streamed through the stained-glass windows in jeweled tones of ruby and emerald and sapphire.

The "guests" stirred in anticipation.

And then, at last, Jenny, on the arm of her "father," slowly walked toward the altar. Simon's heart nearly stopped as he got his first good look at her.

She looked incredible.

She was wearing an old-fashioned dress made of ivory satin trimmed in delicate-looking lace. It had a high collar and long sleeves and a gently flaring skirt that just skimmed the tops of her white satin shoes.

Simon couldn't take his eyes off of her. It was a good thing he was supposed to be watching her, because he couldn't have looked at anything else if he'd wanted to.

Myriad emotions pummeled him. Confusion. Uppermost was incredulity. Had Jenny always looked this beautiful? Had she always been this desirable? And if she had, why hadn't he noticed it before?

As she and her "father" drew abreast of Simon, the actor playing the father placed Jenny's hand in Simon's, then withdrew.

Jenny looked up.

Simon looked down.

And swallowed. Hard.

His heart was beating like a tom-tom.

Her dark eyes were luminous behind the filmy veil. His mouth felt dry. He hoped when it was time to say his "vows" he wouldn't sound like a bullfrog.

The organ stopped playing.

A hush descended over the church.

The lush fragrance of magnolias floated in the air.

The "minister" began speaking.

Simon held on to Jenny's hand and tried to harness his rampaging emotions.

"Do you, Mallory, take this man, Zachary, to be your lawfully wedded husband?" the actor/minister intoned in a deep baritone.

"I do," Jenny said clearly. She smiled at Simon.

The smile was very nearly his undoing.

"Do you, Zachary, take this woman, Mallory, to be your lawfully wedded wife?"

"I—I do," Simon said, and was relieved to hear his voice sound almost normal.

The "minister" smiled benevolently. "I now pronounce you husband and wife." He looked at Simon. "You may kiss the bride."

Simon's hands trembled as he reached for Jenny's veil, lifting it away from her face.

And when his lips touched hers, gently, the way he'd been told to kiss her, something painful clutched at his heart. He suddenly wished things between him and Jenny were different.

He hated this distance between them.

But he felt powerless to change it.

Chapter Ten

After his tumultuous emotional reaction to the church part of the wedding, Simon dreaded the reception part.

And he'd been right to dread it.

The part of the commercial shot at the country club had been sheer torture.

Dancing with Jenny.

Kissing her.

Smiling into her eyes.

Pretending everything was normal, yet knowing their relationship was in shreds.

For over three hours, Simon endured. Now he understood exactly what was meant by the phrase "the agony and the ecstasy," for he vaulted between one or the other of those emotions the entire day.

Would it ever be over? he wondered.

Finally it was.

Simon sighed in relief. The relief was short-lived when he saw Rousseau making a beeline for Jenny. Later, Simon was never sure what had prompted him to do it, but seeing Rousseau heading for Jenny caused every bit of logic to fly out of Simon's head.

Sick of everything, he strode to Jenny's side, reaching her before Rousseau.

Simon grasped her upper arm and bent down and whispered furiously, "Remember what I told you about him," just before Rousseau joined them.

"Jenny, *magnifique!*" Rousseau said. He barely glanced at Simon.

Simon had the wildest desire to punch Rousseau right in the middle of his aristocratic nose. *Magnifique,* he mimicked.

"I have been looking forward to seeing you all week, *chérie,*" Rousseau said. "I hope you're going to be able to have dinner with me this evening."

"She's having dinner with me," Simon said.

Jenny shot him an incredulous look. "Oh? That's news to me," she said, her voice colder than he'd ever heard it.

She turned to Philippe, giving him a dazzling smile. "Simon is mistaken. I am completely free this evening, and I would *love* to have dinner with you."

And then, ignoring Simon, she looped her arm through Rousseau's and they walked off together.

Damn him, damn him, damn him, Jenny fumed.

Oh! She was so mad, she could spit.

Just who did Simon think he was, anyway? How dared he get possessive all of a sudden?

He didn't want her, but he didn't want anyone else to want her, either.

Well, she'd show him!

She would flirt with and go out with anyone she damn well pleased. And she would wear whatever she pleased, too, despite Simon's insulting insinuation a few days ago.

And if Simon didn't like it, he could just go stuff himself!

Throughout the entire evening, Jenny seethed inwardly. Even Philippe's attentiveness, his charm and wit, didn't completely erase the residue of frustration and anger left by Simon's impossible behavior.

She hoped that she'd disguised her inner turmoil. She didn't want Philippe to suspect what was going on.

He didn't seem to, although once or twice during the evening, she caught him looking at her speculatively.

She was grateful when the evening was over and turned down his suggestion of a nightcap. "I'm really tired," she said.

"Yes, I thought perhaps you were," he said kindly.

As they drove to her house, Jenny worried about what she'd do if Philippe tried to kiss her good-night. Although she liked him very much, she didn't think she was ready for anything like that.

Face it, Jenny, as long as you're mooning over Simon, you'll never be ready for anything like that.

To her great relief, Philippe only, kissed her cheek lightly and said, "Thank you for a lovely evening."

"No, thank *you*," Jenny said fervently, trying to assuage the guilt seeping in. Philippe was so *nice*.

If she had any sense at all, she'd encourage him.

* * *

Simon knew what he had to do.

On Monday, if Jenny showed up for their morning run, he would have to apologize and try to get her to understand that what he'd said, he'd only said for her own good.

She didn't show up.

At eleven-thirty, after a less-than-satisfactory morning, Simon put on his suit jacket and headed for the parking garage.

Fifteen minutes later, he pulled into the parking lot of the *Vanguard*.

Five minutes after that, he asked Carla to tell Jenny he was there.

"She said to go on back," the receptionist told him. She batted her eyes at him.

Simon grinned. Carla was an incorrigible flirt. He walked to Jenny's office and knocked on the door.

"Come in," Jenny called.

He took a deep breath and opened the door. She was sitting behind her desk, facing the computer.

She looked around and gave him a little half smile. "Hi. What are you doing here?"

She didn't seem overjoyed to see him, but neither did she seem hostile, he noticed with relief.

He sank into the only other chair in the small room. "I thought we needed to talk."

She swiveled around so she was facing him. "Oh?"

She wasn't going to give him any help. Okay. "Look, I'm sorry if I was overbearing or something the other day, but... I'm worried about you."

A tiny frown line appeared on her forehead. "Oh?" she said again, more slowly this time. "And why is that?"

He'd never realized Jenny could be intimidating if she chose. He guessed there were lots of things about Jenny he hadn't known. He tugged at his tie, which suddenly felt uncomfortably tight. "C'mon, Jenny, let's not play games, okay? We both know you don't have a lot of experience with men. You're pretty naive. And Rousseau is experienced and knows just what buttons to push."

"I see."

Simon hadn't known brown eyes could look cold, but hers sure did. Didn't she see that he was just looking out for her own good? Why was she mad? He was just pointing out the obvious. "Besides, he's old enough to be your father."

Now her eyes flashed fire, and two bright spots of red appeared on her cheeks. "Thank you so much for your concern, Simon," she said in a voice laced with sarcasm. "I really appreciate how much you care about me. It's so gratifying to know that you think I'm naive and stupid and easily flattered, that I have so little experience with men that I can't make my own judgments concerning them."

"Jenny, I just—"

"I'm not finished," she said.

Simon subsided into miserable silence. She wasn't going to be reasonable.

"However," she continued, "you are not my father, and our friendship does not give you the right to tell me how to live my life. I am perfectly capable of making my own decisions."

"I can see it was a mistake to come today," he said, standing.

She stood, too. "Before you go, there's one last thing I want to say. For your information, Philippe is forty-five years old. My father, on the other hand, is sixty-seven years old. You *do* see the difference, don't you?"

Jenny decided Simon was a lost cause. He was dense, impossible, egotistic, arrogant, stupid and infuriating.

As soon as these damned commercials were over, that was it. She was through with him.

Finis. Done. Over. *Sayonara*.

Simon decided Jenny was unreasonable, emotional and irrational.

As soon as these damned commercials were over, maybe she'd finally come to her senses.

He certainly hoped so.

Although the original decision was to begin showing the Hill Country Wines commercials during the first week of the fall television season, Philippe's backers had decided they were sinking too much money into this campaign to shoot any more commercials without testing the market.

They decided to show the first commercial during the broadcast of the Wimbledon tennis matches in early July.

So, for the entire month of June, the cast and crew were on hiatus.

This suited Jenny. Her relationship with Simon was so strained by now that it was no longer fun to do the commercials. And things at work were no better.

She saw very little of Simon in June. He took a two-week vacation and went fly-fishing in Wyoming with his father and uncle.

Jenny spent most of her free time with her family. She refused to think of it as licking her wounds.

Philippe called her several times a week. He invited her to spend a weekend at the winery, but she declined. "Let's wait," she suggested. "I'm very busy right now."

The days marched on.

Finally, it was time for Wimbledon.

Jenny had always imagined she'd watch the first airing of the commercial with Simon. Instead, she was at her parents' home, surrounded by her family, when the big moment came.

Jenny got a lump in her throat seeing how ridiculously happy she looked when she flung open the door and saw Simon on the other side.

And later, when he kissed her, something curled deep inside, and she felt like crying.

Afterward, her family erupted into applause.

"Oh, Jenny, that was *wonderful,*" her mother said. She beamed.

"Now I'm *really* jealous!" Cindy exclaimed, but she hugged Jenny and whispered, "I'm so proud of you, Sissy."

Jenny blinked back tears at the baby nickname.

"Yes, Punkin, you sure were something!" her dad said, pride and love shining in his eyes.

Kate hugged and kissed her. "Hidden depths," she said cryptically.

Only Becky understood what Jenny was feeling. Later, after the family had had shortcake with some of

Lois Randall's home-grown strawberries on top, Becky said, "You and Simon still giving each other the cold shoulder?"

"You could say that."

Becky shook her head. "I think he's in love with you."

Jenny laughed mirthlessly. "He's sure got a funny way of showing it."

Becky's eyes were filled with sympathy. "You okay?"

Jenny sighed. "I'm fine. I've discovered a lot of things about myself in the past couple of months, Beck, and one of them is that I'm very strong. I love Simon, and I wish he loved me, but if he doesn't, I'll survive."

Becky smiled, then enfolded Jenny in a hug. "I'm glad you're my sister," she whispered.

For the second time that day, Jenny blinked back tears. "Thanks. I'm glad, too."

Everywhere Jenny went the next week, people stopped her and congratulated her. The staff at the paper, in particular, seemed starstruck.

Samantha St. James, the host of *Hello, Houston,* a local talk show, called Jenny for an interview.

Clem Bennelli, a reporter for Channel 10, called, wanting to do a local-girl-makes-good piece on her.

Classmates from high school and college called her. People she hadn't thought of in years. Everyone gushed over her. Jenny loved it. She loved it all. The adulation. The envy. The gushing. What was wrong with her? What had happened to her principles?

She thought with chagrin how her friends and family had reacted when she'd won an award for an exposé of a local banker. Her mother had smiled and said, "That's nice, dear." Her sisters had barely noticed. Their lack of understanding and appreciation had really hurt, because she'd been so proud.

And now, now they were treating her with awe and respect. Because she'd starred in a commercial, of all things.

Jenny lapped it all up.

Even Travis-the-jerk, as she now thought of her ex-boyfriend—the one who had dumped her—called.

It gave Jenny the greatest pleasure to tell him, sweetly, of course, to take a flying leap.

Philippe's backers were jubilant. The commercial had been an instant, almost-phenomenal, success.

The sales of Hill Country Wines nearly doubled in the week that followed. Everyone, it seemed, was talking about Zach and Mallory and Hill Country Wines.

Shooting on the remaining commercials would begin again, immediately. To keep Zach and Mallory in the forefront of the audience's consciousness, the first commercial would be repeated weekly until fall, when the second one would appear on a weekly comedy show popular with the chic, young crowd.

The next shoot was scheduled for the following weekend. Jenny wondered how Simon would act. She had gotten over her initial fury concerning his advice about Philippe. Now that she'd gained some distance and perspective, she realized that Simon had probably offered his advice with good intentions. He probably had no idea that he'd sounded condescending and insulting.

She was determined that she would be friendly and pleasant when she saw him, no matter how hard it might be.

On Thursday, Philippe called to say he would come down for the weekend shoot and asked her to have dinner with him on Saturday night.

She accepted, with trepidation.

She knew she had to decide if she wanted to seriously encourage Philippe...and soon. If not, it would not be fair to continue seeing him.

Simon was looking forward to seeing Jenny. He hoped that the time away from each other had healed the breach in their friendship.

He had missed her.

Even the two weeks in Wyoming with his father and uncle, a trip that should have been relaxing and stress-free, hadn't allowed him to completely forget about her.

But he was in pretty good spirits when he arrived at the studio. He felt optimistic that Jenny would have been feeling regrets about their strained relationship, too.

Sure enough, she smiled warmly when she saw him. Relieved, he walked over and put his arm around her shoulders. He hugged her close for a minute. "It's good to see you," he said.

"How was your fishing trip?"

"Great. Boy, Wyoming is beautiful. And it was nice to get away from the heat."

She nodded.

"I missed you," he said impulsively.

Her smile faded, and she gave a funny little shrug. "I missed you, too," she said softly.

There was something in the quality of her voice, something sad, something that made him feel odd. He knew he should say something else, but he wasn't sure what.

Then Dick Craig approached them, and the moment passed. The next time Simon looked for Jenny, she was gone, presumably to her dressing room. He headed off to his.

Later, when he returned to the set, Jenny was back, dressed for the shoot. He looked at her for a long moment. She didn't know he was watching her. She was laughing and talking to Andy, one of the cameramen.

He swallowed.

She was wearing a black strapless dress, short and unbelievably sexy. Big sparkling earrings and very high-heeled shoes added to the provocative look.

Simon wanted to run over and cover her up. He hated the way Andy was ogling her. He looked around. Every man in the place was ogling her. He knew what they were thinking. They were undressing her. Wondering what it would be like to make love to her.

He wanted to punch them all out.

He stood there feeling impotent and frustrated and mad at the world.

A few minutes later, Rousseau arrived.

Simon watched as he greeted Jenny. He clenched his fists as Rousseau bent down to kiss her on one cheek, then the other. He swore under his breath as Rousseau put his arm around her bare shoulders and drew her off to the side where they talked quietly.

He imagined how Jenny's skin felt under Rousseau's fingers. He imagined how she smelled. He imagined how Rousseau's eyes were probably wandering to the little dark cleft between her breasts—the one revealed by the low-cut bodice.

"Shouldn't we get started?" Simon said to Craig, who stood nearby. His voice sounded hoarse.

"Yes," Craig said, giving him an odd look. "Places, everyone," he called.

Before walking onto the set, Simon glanced back at Rousseau and Jenny. She was smiling at him, nodding at something he was saying. Why couldn't she see that the man was all wrong for her? What was it about Rousseau that had dazzled her?

Simon took his place at a small round table set for dinner. The commercial they were shooting today was the one where Zach and Mallory celebrate his first promotion. She fixes a candlelit dinner for two, with flowers and wine. She wears the black dress because it's such a special occasion. At the end of the commercial, Zach lifts her in his arms, and along with the bottle of Hill Country Wine, carries her into the bedroom.

The TV viewers would not see the bedroom, of course, but the inference would be there for them to make.

Simon and Jenny would only share one kiss during this spot. It came in the middle, when they would lean over the little round table where they were eating their dinner.

Jenny finally walked onto the set. She blinked under the bright lights.

Sometimes when Simon looked at her, he couldn't believe it was really her. Where had this Jenny been for the past ten years?

Somehow, Simon managed to get through the commercial. They had to do about a dozen takes before they got it right, but finally, about six o'clock, it was over.

Simon slowly lowered Jenny to the floor. "How about dinner tonight?" he said. "Since you're all dressed up, we could go somewhere like Charley's 517."

"Oh, Simon, I'm sorry. I—I already have dinner plans."

Simon knew who her plans were with. And there wasn't a damned thing he could do about it.

He had to stand there and say it was all right. He had to watch as Rousseau claimed her a few minutes later. He had to endure seeing them leave together.

And for the rest of the night, he had to try to stop his imagination from conjuring torturous images of the two of them sitting close together, maybe even dancing close together. He tried not to think about Rousseau kissing her and touching her.

Because if he did, he would go nuts.

About midway through the evening, Jenny admitted to herself what she had always known. This date with Philippe was a mistake.

"I am worried about my daughter," he confessed. "She needs a woman's influence." He smiled, his dark eyes soft and admiring. "I think she would like you very much. I'm looking forward to introducing you to each other."

Jenny knew at that moment that it wasn't fair to allow him to think she wanted to be the woman in his daughter Giselle's life.

Or his.

Unfortunately, no matter how angry with him she became or how frustrated he made her, Simon was the man she loved. Simon was the man she wanted to spend the rest of her life with.

Jenny knew she would have to tell Philippe she couldn't see him again. She decided she would tell him when he took her home.

But later, when they arrived at her house, before she had a chance to say anything, he drew her into his arms and kissed her.

Jenny didn't push him away.

She couldn't. He was too nice. But she couldn't respond the way she knew he wanted her to.

When he released her, he said slowly, "So that is the way it is."

"I'm sorry, Philippe." She felt like a crud.

"No, no," he said, placing his index finger against her lips. "Do not apologize. It is too soon. I am rushing you."

"No, you're not rushing me. You're such a wonderful man, and I'm flattered by your interest," she said gently, "but it's just not going to work."

"But I thought you said there was no one else."

"There isn't. Not really." Jenny was on the verge of tears. She must be crazy. Most women would kill for the chance to date a man like Philippe Rousseau. "I just... I like you very much, as a friend, but I just don't feel what I should feel for you.''

He nodded. "All right. I won't push you. But I want you to know...if you should change your mind...all you have to do is tell me."

Then he kissed her forehead, said good-night and left.

Jenny walked slowly inside.

And burst into tears.

Chapter Eleven

"All right, places, everyone!" Dick Craig called.

Jenny and Simon took their assigned places on the set—Jenny standing at the sink in the mock kitchen, her back to the door, Simon standing just inside the entrance.

This was the last commercial.

The one where Mallory would tell Zach she was pregnant.

Jenny took a couple of deep breaths in an attempt to calm herself.

The last couple of weeks had been pure hell for her. She'd been a bundle of nerves because of all the tension in her life.

Lately, Jenny thought of her life as a balloon, inexorably filling with air. Any moment now, she expected it to explode around her.

Since the day he had asked her to have dinner with him and she had refused because of her date with Philippe, she had hardly seen Simon. Even their morning runs had fallen by the wayside.

And when she *had* seen him, he acted as if they were working colleagues, nothing more. It was as if their friendship had never been.

In the old days—B.C., as Jenny thought of her life before the commercials—she would simply have said, "This has gone on long enough, Simon. Let's talk about it." Of course, in the old days, nothing like this would have happened.

The strange thing was, the constraint between them did not seem to affect the commercials. Even so, she couldn't squelch the butterflies in her stomach today. She didn't want Simon to know how she was feeling.

"Action!"

Simon reached up to loosen his tie as he walked into the "kitchen."

Jenny turned around, giving him the happy, welcoming smile called for by the script. As always, her heart contracted at the sight of him. "Hi!" she said brightly in her best Mallory voice. "You're home early today. I've barely gotten dinner started."

"Hi, sweetheart," he said, an answering smile on his face. He walked over to the sink and slid his arm around her waist.

Jenny's heart lurched painfully, but she kept her camera smile even, and she hoped her eyes didn't betray her inner turmoil. She turned and lifted her face. Simon kissed her. A sweet rush of love filled her, and even though her hands were wet, and it wasn't in the script, she reached up and clasped his face on either side and tried to tell him with her answering kiss everything that had been in her heart for months, for years.

When they broke apart, confusion clouded his eyes, but he covered it well. His lines sounded natural as he said, "Hey, what's this?" He lifted the bottle of Hill Country Champagne that was chilling in an ice bucket on the counter. "Hill Country Champagne," he added with a low whistle. Then he smiled quizzically. "Special occasion that I don't know about?"

Jenny smiled tremulously. Acting this part was so easy for her. All she did was imagine that it was really her and Simon celebrating their first year of married life. And today, she thought about what bliss it would be to tell Simon she was pregnant with their first child.

"You'd better sit down," she said softly.

He reached for her, pulling her down onto his lap. She looped her arm around his shoulders.

He looked up. His blue eyes were bottomless.

Jenny swallowed. Looking down into his eyes, she remembered so many things. The first time she'd ever seen him. The day his brother was killed and he'd cried in her arms. Their celebratory dinner the night Alonzo and Christopher had landed the Western Oil account. All of the confidences they'd shared. The years of friendship and love between them.

She wanted to cry.

What had happened to them?

Blinking back her tears, she smiled and said, "Zach." Her voice sounded wobbly, just the way it was supposed to. "I—I have something to tell you."

His arms tightened around her. His eyes searched hers.

"What is it, darling?"

The endearment was meant for Mallory. Jenny knew that. And yet, hearing the word on his lips caused the most agonizing, bittersweet pain to knife through her. "I went to the doctor today," she said softly. "He gave me some wonderful news." *Oh, Simon, Simon, I love you so much. Can't you feel it? Can't you see it?*

"Mallory! Are . . . are you saying?"

She nodded her head. "Yes, sweetheart, yes. We're going to have a baby!"

He stood, bringing her with him. He held her tightly for a moment, smiling down into her eyes. "I'm the luckiest man in the world." He kissed her gently.

"There's just one bad part," she said when he lifted his head.

He frowned. "What's that?"

Jenny laughed. "I sure am going to miss my Hill Country Wine!"

"Cut!" Craig yelled. "That was perfect! Perfect!"

The crew milled around them, congratulating them, slapping Simon on the back. Several people kissed Jenny. Everyone was in a festive mood.

"Hey," a cameraman called, "let's open that bottle of wine!"

"Good idea," someone else said.

"I have more in my car," Philippe said, joining them on the set. He walked straight over to Jenny and Simon. In his arms was an enormous bouquet of flowers. He smiled at Simon and said, "Congratulations, Simon. Excellent work."

Then he turned to Jenny. With a little bow, he presented her with the flowers. "For you, Jenny. With my thanks and undying admiration."

Jenny could feel her face heating as the entire crew began to clap and cheer.

"Speech, speech," someone called.

"Stop it," she said, knowing she'd turned the color of a lobster.

"Listen, everyone," Philippe said, "I told Dick I wanted to hold the wrap party at my home this weekend. You're all invited."

There were more cheers, and Philippe smiled at her. Jenny smiled back, but as soon as Philippe's attention was diverted by a question from one of the crew, her eyes searched for the person whose approval meant more to her than anyone's and always would.

She found Simon, but he wasn't smiling. He wasn't even looking at her.

He was walking off the set. All she saw was the back of his head.

A moment later, he was gone.

If she wanted a man like Philippe Rousseau, she could have him. Simon sure as hell didn't care. Lord! Simon couldn't believe that sappy display, and he had no intention of sticking around for more.

And it wasn't just Rousseau.

Every one of the crew members, especially the *male* crew members, acted besotted by Jenny. They fawned all over her, just the way Rousseau did.

The thing that really galled Simon was Jenny's reaction. It was obvious she loved it!

He couldn't believe it. Jenny. The same Jenny who had always made so much fun of his Barbie dolls was now acting like one herself! If Simon hadn't been so disgusted, he would have laughed at the irony.

The hell with her.

The hell with all of them.

The hell with everything.

He climbed into his Vette, jammed the key into the ignition and roared out of the parking lot. Gravel spewed behind him.

Forty-five minutes later, in the shadowy confines of his living room, he was well on his way to getting totally, thoroughly, and very satisfyingly drunk.

And *not* on Hill Country Wine, either!

Simon's behavior mystified Jenny. What in the world was going on with him? His actions all suggested he was jealous. Yet he had made no move toward her, no attempt to stake his claim—if staking his claim was what he desired.

What was she to think?

What was she to do?

It was the Thursday after their final shoot, and this weekend was the wrap party at Philippe's home. Simon had not called all week, nor had he shown up at the track.

Jenny pondered calling him dozens of times, but she felt weird about doing so in the face of his behavior. She sighed. She had so hoped Simon would call and suggest they drive to the winery together.

But he hadn't, so she'd decided to fly to Austin and take Philippe up on his offer to pick her up at the Austin airport. She'd made her reservations this morning. She wished she felt more enthusiastic about the trip and the party. Shoot, she wished she felt more enthusiastic about everything.

She sighed again and stretched. Boy, she was tired! She'd been sitting at her computer all afternoon. She knew she shouldn't do that. Her doctor had told her long ago that eyestrain and back and shoulder problems would be her constant companions if she didn't get up and walk around at least once every hour.

She glanced at her watch. Good grief! It was after five. Where had the time gone?

Well, she only had a paragraph or two to finish her story. She might as well stay until it was done.

But first she needed to visit the ladies' room.

She walked through the deserted production area. On Wednesdays and Thursdays, only Pete and one or two of the production people worked at all, and even they were long gone. In fact, the entire place was quiet. Maybe she was the last one here.

The ladies' room door was closed.

She knocked, thinking maybe someone had just closed the door by mistake and the room was really empty.

There was no answer, so she reached for the knob. It wouldn't turn.

Since the ladies' room was occupied, she wandered back out to the production area and touched her toes a few times, then did some head and shoulder rolls.

That felt good. She hadn't realized just how stiff she was. She glanced back toward the ladies' room. Whoever was in there was certainly taking a long time.

Idly, she wandered around the room.

Two minutes went by, then three. She frowned.

Could something be wrong in there?

She walked back to the ladies' room and knocked again. Hard. "Are you all right in there?" she called.

"J-just a minute," said a muffled voice.

Jenny waited patiently. Finally, the door opened, and a red-eyed, puffy-faced Emma Goodman walked out.

"Emma," she said, shocked to see the normally cheerful bookkeeper so obviously distraught. "What's wrong?"

Emma's lower lip trembled, and she blinked rapidly behind her trifocals. Her eyes filled with fresh tears.

"Oh, Emma," Jenny said. She drew the older woman into her arms. "Come here. Sit down." Leading Emma to one of the desks, Jenny pulled out a chair and made her sit.

Emma produced a handkerchief and, removing her glasses, wiped her eyes. Then she blew her nose. "I—I'm s-sorry."

"No, don't be sorry! Just tell me what's wrong," Jenny said. She sat on the desk and patted Emma's shoulder. She could feel how the woman was trembling. Oh, God, had something happened to one of her children or grandchildren? Surely not. *Oh, please, God, surely not!*

"I—I...he..." Emma swallowed. "He fired me," she whispered.

"He *fired* you?" Jenny said incredulously. "*Who* fired you? Bob?"

Emma bit her bottom lip, tears forming again. She swallowed, then nodded her head.

Shock zinged through Jenny, followed on its heels by a fury so strong, it caused her heart to slam against her chest wall. "Bob fired you," she repeated. "Why?"

Emma's face crumpled. "H-he said I was too slow. Th-that I made t-too many mistakes. He s-said he was...s-sorry, but things were...were changing... and I didn't fit in any longer. Oh, Jenny," she said, moaning, "what am I going to do? Nobody wants an old...old woman like me...."

Jenny's teeth were clenched so hard, she was afraid she'd chip the enamel. She knew, from subtle hints Emma had dropped along the way, that the older woman probably needed the money her salary provided. And she was right. Who *would* hire someone her age? Although it infuriated Jenny to admit it, the world was not fair, and age discrimination *did* exist.

Jenny comforted Emma as best she could. Then she helped her pack up her belongings and take them out to her car. All the while, she cast angry looks in the direction of Bob's office. Boy, she would have a few choice things to say to him once Emma was safely out of earshot.

"I'll call you later," Jenny promised after kissing Emma's cheek. "You sure you'll be all right driving home?"

Emma nodded. "I'll be fine. I'm okay now. It—it was just such a shock."

"I know."

"Thank you, Jenny. You're a wonderful friend."

The taillights of Emma's car were barely out of the parking lot before Jenny was striding back into the building and heading straight for Bob's office.

She rapped on the closed door sharply.

"Yes?"

She opened the door.

He had his hand over the mouthpiece of the phone. "Yes?" he said again. His eyes were cool. Their relationship had been strained ever since Jenny had refused to attend the benefit luncheon.

"I need to talk to you," she said between tight lips.

He waved her to a seat, then uncovered the receiver. "Keith? Can I call you back later?"

He smiled, said his goodbyes to the unknown Keith, then hung up the phone. "Well," he said, "what can I do for you?"

"You fired Emma," Jenny said.

A muscle in his jaw twitched. "Regrettably, yes, I had to let her go."

"But why? She's a wonderful employee. She's loyal and hardworking and completely dependable." She had to hold on to her temper. She knew she wouldn't get anywhere with him if she attacked him.

"It was strictly a business decision."

"A business decision! But Emma's been a part of this business for almost its entire existence. She knows the paper inside out. You'll never be able to replace her with anyone better."

He leaned back in his chair and tented his hands, studying her over the tops of them. "I don't expect you to understand. You're not privy to certain facts. However, I can't let sentimentality overrule my business judgment. Emma Goodman's way of working is old-fashioned and inefficient. I plan to replace her with a computerized bookkeeping system. It's too bad, but Emma is a luxury we can no longer afford—"

"No longer afford!" Jenny jumped up. "How can you treat people that way? Don't you have any decency, any scruples, any sense of fair—"

"I don't care for your tone of voice," he said, interrupting her tirade. "And I don't remember asking for your opinion. It was my decision to make, and I made it. Now, if you don't mind, I'm very busy." He picked up the phone and punched in some numbers, ignoring her.

Jenny glared at him. She knew she had two choices, well, three. She could keep haranguing him, which would probably get *her* fired, too. She could leave and try to do something for Emma on her own. Or she could quit.

She stood there indecisively, torn between the urge to tell him to take his job and shove it and the more sensible course of leaving before she did anything irrevocable.

Her good sense won out.

She shot him one more furious glare, wasted because he still wasn't looking at her, then turned on her heel and marched out, head high.

She *did* give in to the childish urge to slam the door behind her. It didn't make her feel better.

Later, at home, when she'd calmed down, she called Emma. "Let's go out to dinner tonight," she said, falsely cheerful. "We can talk about everything, see if we can come up with a plan."

"Oh, Jenny, you're so sweet to ask me, but I'm all right, really I am."

Emma did sound better. Calmer and more accepting. Almost like her old self. "I know you're all right," Jenny insisted, "but I *want* to take you out."

"I really can't go tonight. Tilly's coming over." Tilly was Emma's double cousin. Jenny had heard all about her for years. Their fathers had been brothers and their mothers had been sisters, and Emma and Tilly had grown up living next door to each other in the Heights. Even now, they only lived a block apart.

"Well, in that case..." Damn. If only she were going to be here this weekend. "If you're sure you're all right...maybe we could do it on Monday?" Oh, shoot, on Monday she'd be working late. "Well, I guess it would have to be Tuesday."

"Don't worry about me, Jenny. I'm sorry I was such a crybaby earlier. I'm fine. In fact, Tilly and I have talked, and we've decided that I should sell my house and move in with her. With that and my social security, I'll be in good shape." She laughed, and her laugh sounded almost, but not quite, like the old Emma. "Who knows? I may even enjoy being a lady of leisure!"

Jenny sat and looked at the phone for a long time after they'd hung up. She felt unutterably sad. Poor Emma. Jenny wondered what she should do. If only she had someone she could talk to about all of this. She smiled ruefully. *Who are you kidding? You don't want to talk to just anybody. You want to talk to Simon.*

If she could only call him. Discussing problems with him always made everything seem brighter, always put things into perspective. But she couldn't. Not now. Not when he was acting the way he was. She dropped her head into her hands. Oh, God. Everything was such a mess!

She didn't sleep well that night, and the following day was awful. The entire staff tiptoed around, whispered in corners and generally cast wary eyes at their co-workers. Several times during the day, people slipped into her office to say, "Jenny, isn't it awful?"

Jenny knew they were genuinely concerned about Emma. She also knew they were scared that they would be next.

Finally, the day was over.

She couldn't wait to get out of there. She was booked on an eight-o'clock flight out of Hobby Airport and she still had to pack. She'd been too upset last night to do anything more than pace restlessly. Thinking about the upcoming trip to the winery, she realized she hadn't even told anyone in her family that she'd be gone for the weekend. She reached for the phone to call Becky. At that moment, it rang.

She picked up the receiver. "Jenny Randall."

"Hello, Miss Randall. My name is Gail Terno, and I'm with the Russell Brown Agency in Los Angeles."

"Yes?" Jenny said cautiously. Who and what was the Russell Brown Agency?

"You don't know me, but our agency worked with Dick Craig Productions on a project last fall, and he told me how to reach you."

"Oh."

"Sunshine Swimwear is a client of ours," Gail Terno continued.

Sunshine Swimwear was a name Jenny recognized. Any woman over the age of sixteen would recognize it, because they were the most popular maker of women's swimwear and resort wear in the country.

"Lucy Calvin, the owner of Sunshine, saw you in the Hill Country Wine commercial and wants you for Sunshine's new ad campaign."

"Me?" Jenny squeaked.

Terno's chuckle sounded hearty and sincere. "Don't act so surprised. You're wonderful in the Hill Country ad. The whole country's caught up in the story of Zach and Mallory."

Jenny smiled. She would have had to be made of stone not to feel pleased by the woman's compliment. "Thank you."

"The Sunshine ads will be shot on St. James Island in the Caribbean," Terno said. "We'd like to start filming no later than September first, but mid-August would be even better. We anticipate being on location for three weeks to a month." Before Jenny could say anything, Terno added, "I know you have another job, that you're not a model or an actress by profession, but I was hoping you could take vacation or a leave of absence, or something." She waited a heartbeat. "The job pays fifty thousand dollars."

Jenny very nearly stopped breathing. Fifty thousand dollars! Nearly two years' salary at the paper. For one month's work. "I—I don't know what to say."

"Say yes."

Jenny exhaled slowly. "Would...would I be wearing swimsuits?"

"Yes, for one of the ads. In another, you'd be photographed with a bikini top and a sarong-type skirt on the bottom."

"But I thought swimwear models had to be really thin."

Terno laughed. "No. In fact, this is the one time it's an advantage to have a more lush figure. Not that you're fat, but you've got a nicely rounded, athletic figure that will show well in our ads."

"I—I hardly know what to say."

"I know this comes as a surprise to you, and I don't want to rush you into anything. Take a few days to think it over, then call me."

After they'd hung up, Jenny sat there, stunned. Gail Terno had agreed to give Jenny the weekend to mull over the offer. Jenny was to call her Monday morning and give her her answer.

Boy, it was tempting. It was very tempting. But how could she accept? She would have to quit her job if she took this assignment, because she didn't have a month's vacation to take. In fact, all she had left was one week.

And after what had happened yesterday, she sure wasn't going to ask Hennessey for a leave of absence as Gail Terno had suggested. No way. Not that he would give her one, even if she did ask. Even before their confrontation over Emma, Jenny hadn't exactly been his favorite person. In fact, he was probably just looking for a good excuse to get rid of her, too.

Jenny closed her eyes.

What should she do?

For at least the tenth time in the last twenty-four hours, she desperately wanted to call Simon. She had to talk to him. Somehow, she had to overcome the barrier between them. She didn't want to make a decision like this one on her own.

Actually, though, this news was too important to discuss on the phone. If she was going to talk to him, it would be better to do it in person. She wanted to see his face and the expression in his eyes when she told him about this job offer.

Yes, that made sense, she thought with relief. She would talk to him face-to-face. This weekend, she'd find an opportunity to be alone with him and she would make him talk to her, whether he wanted to or not.

Feeling better, she shut off her computer.

A second later, there was a tap on her door.

What now? she thought wearily. "Come in."

She nearly groaned aloud when she saw that her visitor was Bob Hennessey.

"About this editorial of yours," he said without preamble as he walked into her office. He tapped a strip of typeset copy.

"What about it?" Jenny stood behind her desk. Maybe if she continued to stand, he would get this over with fast.

"I want you to write something else."

"Why? What's wrong with that one? I think it's one of the best editorials I've ever written."

"This," he said disdainfully, "attacks billboards."

"Yes, I know."

"You should also know that one of our biggest advertisers is Joe's Boards."

"So?" Did he think she was going to shake in her boots just because an advertiser might not like what she'd written? Fat chance.

"So I don't think this editorial is appropriate."

"Well, I'm sorry you feel that way, Bob," she said firmly, "but I don't agree. The billboard situation in West U has reached crisis proportions. They're an eyesore, and it's time we did something about them.'' *You don't live here, so you don't care,* she wanted to add, *but we do.* "Gloria and I discussed this story before she left, and she gave me the go-ahead.''

"Gloria no longer owns this paper.''

"Oh, I'm well aware of *that.*'' She knew her voice dripped with sarcasm, but she didn't care.

"And Joe's Boards just signed a yearlong contract with us—a contract Walker fought to get.''

Jenny shrugged. Walker, their top salesman, wasn't her concern. Nor was Boards. Editorial was her concern. It was also her exclusive domain. And she'd be damned if she'd allow some number cruncher who fired sixty-three-year-old ladies to dictate editorial policy to her.

"I do not want to offend a new advertiser.''

"You don't want to offend *any* advertiser,'' Jenny countered.

"Yes, that's true. But it would be particularly bad policy to get off on the wrong foot with someone new.''

Jenny stared at him.

Maybe, if circumstances were different, she would be willing to pull the editorial. Maybe, if this were Gloria, Jenny would compromise. Maybe, if gorgeous Bob hadn't fired Emma so heartlessly, Jenny might feel more reasonable.

But this wasn't Gloria.

And he *had* fired Emma.

And Jenny hated him.

Of course, Gloria never would have asked Jenny to pull the story in the first place. Gloria would have backed Jenny's decision, one hundred percent.

She dug in her heels.

"That's the editorial I wrote for this week's paper, and that's the editorial I plan to run. Now, if you'll excuse me, it's past my quitting time, and I've got a plane to catch."

Chapter Twelve

At six-thirty, Simon picked up the phone and called Jenny. The line was busy.

At seven o'clock, he called again.

He frowned when he heard her answering machine kick in. He left a message asking her to call him when she got home.

At nine o'clock, when he hadn't heard from her, he called again. He got the answering machine.

He got it again at ten o'clock.

And again at eleven o'clock.

He slammed down the receiver and said a few choice cusswords. Either she was ignoring his messages and pretending not to be home, or she wasn't home.

And if she wasn't home, where the hell was she?

On a date?

Or had she gone to the winery early? Was she even now in the company of Philippe Rousseau?

Morosely, Simon thought about how only a few months ago, he would have known exactly where she was and what she was doing. Today he hadn't a clue.

He had been going to suggest they ride to the winery together tomorrow morning. He had hoped that during the long drive, they might begin to patch up their differences. Repair their friendship. Make a new beginning.

You should have asked her sooner, a taunting inner voice chided.

He picked up a book that was lying on his coffee table and threw it across the room. It made a satisfying *whummmp* as it landed against the far wall.

He was mad at the world, but he was even madder at himself. He didn't know what was wrong with him lately, but he seemed to do nothing right, especially where Jenny was concerned.

He slumped down onto the couch and stared at his feet.

It was going to be a long weekend.

Every time Jenny looked in Simon's direction, Giselle Rousseau was less than two feet away, hanging on to his every word. This was the way it had been for the entire weekend, ever since Simon had arrived at noon.

The fifteen-year-old obviously had a gigantic crush on him. Ordinarily, Jenny wouldn't have minded the teenager dogging his footsteps. In fact, Jenny would have been gently amused by the girl's slavish devotion. After all, Jenny knew what it was like to feel that way about Simon.

This weekend, though, Jenny wasn't feeling very charitable.

She wanted to talk to Simon.

Alone.

All day she tried to corner him.

All day she was unsuccessful.

She tried to enjoy herself. She had been looking forward to seeing the winery, and she deserved to celebrate the conclusion of the filming. If only she and Simon could talk, maybe then she could relax.

By Saturday night, after a delicious dinner of roasted quail, Jenny was more than a little frustrated. She was sure she would be able to get him all to herself once Giselle had gone to bed, for surely a fifteen-year-old wouldn't be allowed to stay up as long as the adults.

Jenny was right about that.

Giselle said good-night a little after eleven.

But by then Simon had been persuaded to join a poker game with four of the men, and after watching them play until well past midnight, Jenny realized the game was going to go into the wee hours.

Reluctantly, she said her own good-nights. Simon barely glanced at her.

The next morning, she awoke early. She knew brunch would be served at ten, but Philippe had said that coffee and rolls would be available from seven o'clock on.

Jenny showered and dressed for the day in a pale yellow cotton sundress and sandals. Then she quietly descended the stairs. Coffee smells wafted through the air, and she followed her nose, heading in the direction of the kitchen.

When she entered the sunlit room with its cool tiled floors and open-beamed ceiling, Philippe was already there. He stood with his back to her. He had a coffee cup in his right hand, and he was looking out the window.

As Jenny walked farther into the room, she saw that there was a bird feeder mounted outside the window, and a pair of cardinals were feeding.

Philippe turned at her footsteps. He smiled, his dark eyes soft as they rested on her face. "Good morning."

"Good morning." Jenny headed straight for the coffeepot. "That coffee sure smells good." She poured herself a mugful, added a dollop of cream and a packet of sweetener. After stirring, she took a sip. It tasted wonderful. "Am I the first one up?"

"Besides me, yes," Philippe said. He turned to face her, leaning casually against the counter.

He looked particularly handsome this morning, Jenny thought, in light summer pants and a dark cotton shirt open at the throat.

"You should wear yellow more often," he said, his eyes frankly admiring. "It's a very good color for you."

Jenny shifted uncomfortably. She wished she hadn't come down so early. She wished someone else was up and in the kitchen with them. She knew Philippe still hoped she would change her mind about him, but it was never going to happen. "Thank you."

"Shall we take our coffee outside to the terrace?" he said.

"All right." She followed him to the back door and walked through as he held it open for her.

Outside, the early-morning air smelled fresh and felt pleasantly cool on her skin. Dew silvered the lawn and the acres of vineyards stretching as far as the eye could see. Although it was early August, and in Houston it would be sweltering and humid, here in the hills the temperature was at least ten degrees cooler.

Jenny walked to the edge of the terrace and looked around. "It's so beautiful here," she said as Philippe walked up behind her. "You have a lovely home."

"Thank you."

She could feel him behind her, but she didn't turn around.

"I have loved having you here this weekend, you know that, don't you?" His voice was soft.

"It's been a wonderful party," Jenny said casually, purposely misunderstanding his meaning. "Everyone's having a great time."

"That isn't what I meant."

Jenny sighed, finally turning to face him. She looked up into his kind eyes. "I know."

He studied her for a long moment. Then he smiled sadly. "It's not going to work, is it? No matter how patient I am, you're not going to change your mind about me."

Jenny shook her head slowly. "I'm sorry, Philippe."

He shrugged. "Ah, well . . ."

Jenny decided he was too nice not to give him an explanation. "The truth is, I'm in love with someone else, even though he doesn't feel the same way about me."

Philippe nodded thoughtfully. "I guessed as much."

Jenny frowned. "You did?"

"Yes, and don't be so sure he doesn't love you."

"Are we talking about the same person?" Jenny said glumly. "The same one who's been ignoring me all weekend?"

Philippe smiled. "The ways of men are sometimes hard to fathom, Jenny."

"You're so nice, Philippe. I wish I did love you."

"Not as much as I wish it, *chérie.*"

They smiled at each other. He set his coffee mug on a nearby wrought-iron table. Then, gently, he drew her into his arms, kissing her softly. "Be happy, lovely Jenny," he murmured.

Jenny touched his cheek. Tears burned at the backs of her eyes. "I'll try," she whispered.

They stood that way, smiling at each other, for a long moment. Then, sighing, Jenny drained her coffee cup. "I think I'll go in and get another cup."

"I'll go with you."

Jenny turned to reenter the house. Then she stopped dead. Her gaze collided with Simon's. Simon—who stood in the open doorway with a thunderous look in his eyes.

Simon took a gulp of coffee, walked to the sink, poured out the rest and rinsed his cup. He kept his back to Jenny and Rousseau, who had walked inside. He tried to empty his mind of the turmoil and pain that had slammed into him when he'd walked to the open back door and unexpectedly encountered Rousseau kissing Jenny.

He carefully placed his cup on the drain board, then slowly turned toward them. He had managed to squash his chaotic emotions temporarily. He was determined not to let them know how much their kissy-face act had rocked him.

"Glad I caught you," he said to Rousseau while carefully avoiding eye contact with Jenny. "I wanted to thank you for the party. It was great."

"Are you leaving?" Rousseau said, clearly surprised.

"Yeah, I thought I'd get an early start back. Got a busy week ahead."

"But, Simon, you'll miss brunch," Jenny said.

Simon finally let his eyes meet hers. "I'm not hungry."

He saw her swallow, saw the slight hunching of her shoulders—an oddly vulnerable movement that he refused to allow to sway him. She had made her choice. She had not listened to one word of the advice he had given her. Well, fine. But if she thought he was going to stick around and watch her and Rousseau make goo-goo eyes at each other, she had another think coming.

He turned to Rousseau. He stuck out his right hand. Rousseau took it, and they shook, exchanged a few more meaningless pleasantries, and then Simon gave Jenny one parting glance. "See you in Houston," he said.

"See you," she echoed, her eyes unhappy.

He refused to feel guilty. It wasn't his fault their friendship was in tatters. She was the one who had changed. Not him.

An hour later, he was on his way, driving with the top down through the hot August morning at a speed that probably wasn't safe but certainly felt therapeutic to his bruised ego and his equally bruised heart.

Bob Seger's "Still the Same" rocked from the speakers.

Over and over, the scene from the terrace played in his mind. Rousseau's hand lying possessively on Jenny's shoulder. The way she'd smiled at him. The way she'd tipped her face up for his kiss.

Simon's heart went *thump, thump, thump* as he remembered how Rousseau's lips had covered hers.

You're a fool. You're a dumb, stupid fool.

Why did he care, anyway? What was it to him if Jenny wanted Rousseau? Big deal! Let her have him! Let them have each other! Who cared?

Dust flew up in billows as he careered down the narrow country road leading to the main highway that would take him to Interstate 10 and home.

After a miserable, nearly sleepless night, Jenny dragged herself into work on Monday morning. She'd realized, along about four o'clock in the morning, that she wasn't going to be able to discuss the problem of Emma or anything else with Simon. That meant that as far as the modeling assignment went, she would have to make her decision on her own.

Simon obviously did not want to talk to her, even before the fiasco Sunday morning.

He had seen Philippe kiss her, and he hadn't liked what he'd seen. That, too, was obvious.

What Simon's reaction meant, she had no idea. For all she knew, he could just be ticked off because she'd ignored his advice about Philippe. Her earlier idea that he was jealous might be completely mistaken.

Jenny rubbed her forehead wearily. Only eight forty-five, and her head was splitting already. She dumped her belongings in her office and headed for the coffeemaker. After pouring herself a cup, she walked into the production area and wandered over to the long slanted tables where the page layouts for this week's paper were in various stages of completion.

She looked at the front page. Most of the stories were already pasted up. The front page looked good. Thelma, her assistant, wrote the headlines.

Slowly, sipping her coffee, she glanced over the second page.

Then her eyes landed on the third page—the editorial page. She stared. Blinked. Looked closer.

Her billboard editorial wasn't there.

In its place was some innocuous story about a school-board meeting. She whirled so fast, coffee sloshed over the rim of her cup and splattered her denim skirt.

She charged out of the room and down the hall, looking for Thelma. She found her in the sales bull pen, talking to a new salesman.

"Thelma, what happened to my billboard editorial?" Jenny said, breaking into their conversation.

Thelma turned, her eyes round with surprise. "Oh, hi, Jenny."

"What happened to my billboard editorial?" Jenny repeated.

"Uh, Bob pulled it."

Jenny's eyes narrowed. "I see." She swung on her heel and stalked off in the direction of Bob Hennessey's office. His door was shut. Without knocking, she opened it.

He was sitting behind his desk, head bent over some papers. He looked up. Frowned. Opened his mouth to say something.

"You decided not to run the billboard editorial," Jenny stated flatly.

"Yes." His blue-green eyes met hers evenly. Their expression clearly said, *Do you want to make something of it?*

Jenny took a deep breath. "In that case, I quit. Do you want me to give you two weeks' notice, or do you want me to leave now?"

He stared at her for a long moment. The brass clock on his credenza chimed the hour. "Maybe it's best if you leave now."

"Fine."

It took Jenny only thirty minutes to clean out her desk and pack up her belongings in a small cardboard box. Then she slowly walked around and said her goodbyes.

Shocked faces, stunned expressions and startled exclamations greeted her news.

"Oh, Jenny," Megan said, looking up from a chart she'd been working on. She got up, came around her desk and gave Jenny a hard hug. "Keep in touch."

"I will," Jenny promised, a lump in her throat. She would miss Megan.

"Hey, kid, onward and upward," Pete said. He hugged her, too. "I'm gonna miss you, though."

"I'll miss you, too." The lump got bigger.

He leaned closer, whispering in her ear, "I've got some feelers out. I'll keep you posted."

She nodded.

"Gee, Jenny, it won't be the same without you," Carla said. Her pretty gray eyes looked miserable.

Jenny gave the receptionist a resigned smile and squeezed her shoulders. "Thanks."

"Who am I gonna talk to about all the latest movies?" Karen, the typesetter, said.

Thelma had tears in her eyes. "I wish you weren't going, Jenny," she said.

Jenny nodded. She didn't trust herself to speak.

Finally, the goodbyes were over. Jenny removed the door key from her key ring and gave it to Carla. Pete carried the cardboard box out to her car.

She turned and looked at the building. Seven years. She'd spent the last seven years of her life here. The *Vanguard* had meant so much to her. Gloria, Megan, Pete, Emma, all the people who'd come and gone, so many memories crowded in on her.

Tears blurred her eyes. It was hard to believe that she would never walk through the front door again, never cover another story, never write another editorial.

How could something so good end so abruptly and so badly?

She took a deep, shaky breath and climbed into her car.

By ten-thirty, she was halfway home.

The first thing she did when she reached the house was call Gail Terno in Los Angeles. "Do you still want me for the Sunshine Swimwear ads?"

"Absolutely.

"Good. I accept your offer."

"That's great! Miss Calvin will be so pleased."

They talked for a while, with Terno filling Jenny in on more details of the job.

After she hung up, Jenny sat by the phone and thought. And thought. Then she called Simon's agency. "Simon," she said when they were connected, "it's Jenny."

"Is something wrong?" His voice sounded cautious.

"Not exactly. But there is something I want to discuss with you."

"All right." Now his voice sounded a little warmer. "How about lunch?"

"Why don't you come over here tonight instead?"

"Don't you have to work tonight?"

"No."

"Well, sure, I can come over. What time?"

They agreed that he would come at seven.

"I'll pick up some Chinese, okay?"

Jenny smiled. Chinese. It was almost like old times. "Great."

At six, she took a bubble bath.

At six-thirty, she began dressing. Now that she'd taken the plunge and called Simon, she had decided to go for broke, put everything on the line tonight.

One of her mother's favorite sayings floated through her mind: God helps those who help themselves. Well, Jenny intended to give herself every bit of help she could manage.

She put on the raspberry dress and matching high-heeled pumps. She took pains with her hair and her makeup, just as Laine had shown her. When she was finished, she studied herself in the mirror.

She looked as good as it was possible for her to look, she decided. She just hoped it was good enough. She crossed her fingers. Simon's reaction to her news would tell her whether there was any hope for them at all.

When her front doorbell rang just a few minutes past seven, she took several deep breaths, and murmured a quick prayer as she hurried to answer the door.

Simon had been in an agony of anticipation all day long. Jenny had sounded so serious when she'd said she needed to talk to him.

What was she going to say?

Fear seized him several times.

What if she told him she was engaged to Rousseau? Surely she wouldn't be. Surely she would never go that far. Surely she would eventually realize the man was all wrong for her.

But what if she didn't?

Well, he would just have to handle it, that's all.

He dressed carefully for the evening. Khaki pants. Dark blue cotton shirt. Brown loafers.

He even shaved again and splashed on cologne. He wasn't sure why.

At six-thirty, he headed for the Chinese place.

At six forty-five, food on the passenger seat, he pointed his Vette in the direction of Jenny's house.

As he stood on the front stoop, he hesitated for a moment before ringing the bell. He felt as nervous and jittery as a teenager going on his first date. Why, he didn't know. It was just Jenny, for Pete's sake! He took several deep breaths, then pressed the doorbell.

A second later, the door opened.

Jenny smiled up at him. "Hi," she said softly.

"Hi."

She looked . . . beautiful. There was no other word for it. She was wearing the dark red dress she'd worn in their first commercial. The color was perfect for her. Her hair curled softly around her face, and her eyes were shining.

Simon's heart beat harder as he walked inside. The light, flowery perfume she wore drifted in the air around him, making him feel almost light-headed.

As they walked to the kitchen, he said, "Paper must have been small this week."

"Huh?" She turned, a tiny frown between her eyes.

He smiled, his jitters suddenly gone. The look on her face was so familiar. *She* was so familiar. Why had he been nervous, anyway? "I said, the paper must have really been small this week. Since you're done so early."

She made a face.

By now they were in the kitchen, and he dumped the bag of food on the table. "Something *is* wrong," he said.

"I quit my job," she said.

Simon gawked at her. "You *what?*"

She smiled ruefully and nodded. "I quit. You know, *el terminato.*"

"What happened?"

"Sit down, and I'll tell you about it. You want some iced tea?"

"Sure."

She busied herself pouring two glasses of tea. The table was already set. Several big serving spoons sat in the middle, along with a bottle of soy sauce. He started opening the cartons of food.

As they served themselves, she told him about the episode that had happened on Friday, right before she'd left for the wrap party at the winery.

At the mention of the party, Simon frowned. He didn't want to think about the party. He especially didn't want to think about Philippe Rousseau.

He forced himself to concentrate on what she was saying.

"Anyway, Hennessey told me I might be happier somewhere else, and I agreed." Jenny grimaced, then speared a piece of fried dumpling on her fork. "I really didn't think he would pull the story, though."

"Are you sorry you quit?" Jenny had loved her job so much. He knew it couldn't have been easy for her to walk out.

She chewed slowly, considering. Finally, she sighed. "No, not really. I'm sorry about the *way* it ended, though. I was there a long time. There are a lot of good memories. The paper really meant something to me."

"I know."

"But it's not the same paper anymore. Since Gloria left, Hennessey's been making changes. Some subtle. Some not so subtle." She looked at him, her dark eyes serious. "He fired Emma Thursday."

Simon stared. "He fired Emma! Why?"

"He said she was *inefficient*. What he really meant was *expendable*," she said bitterly. "He plans to replace her with a computerized bookkeeping system. Can you believe it?"

"No, I can't. Why, Emma was practically a fixture at the paper. And, from what you've said, I thought she was a terrific worker."

Jenny smiled cynically. "She was."

"What's she going to do?"

"She says she's going to sell her house and move in with Tilly."

Simon smiled. "The famous Tilly."

Jenny smiled, too. "She'll be all right, I hope."

"If she's a good bookkeeper, she can probably find another job."

"Simon," Jenny chided. "She's sixty-three, almost sixty-four. Be serious."

He nodded thoughtfully. "You're probably right."

He ate some of his Cashew Chicken and thought about how far apart they'd drifted in the past weeks. Before they'd started shooting the commercials, if something this important had happened, he would have been the first person she called. Feeling deep regret for the chasm that had developed between them, he met her gaze. "Jenny, I'm sorry."

She shrugged. "It's not your fault."

"I meant that I'm sorry I wasn't here when you needed me."

Her warm, dark eyes studied him for a long moment. "Well, anyway, after the Emma thing, I was already fed up, and then, when I got into work today, he'd pulled the story, and that did it."

Simon had figured as much.

"So I marched into his office and quit on the spot."

"And you didn't give him any notice?"

"I offered, but he told me he'd rather I left today. So I did." She wiped her mouth with her napkin, then crumpled it and threw it down on her plate. "You know, I've been thinking about this, and I think Bob has wanted to get rid of me from the very first."

"Why would he want that? For God's sake, you're an award-winning journalist. And you're cheap."

She laughed. "You couldn't resist saying that, could you?"

He was glad he'd made her smile. He hated what had happened to her. Even though it was her decision to quit, she'd been forced into it. He wished she'd been able to make this same decision simply because she recognized it was time for her to move forward with her life.

"So what do you plan to do now?" he said. "Look for a job with another newspaper?"

"Well...that's what I wanted to talk to you about."

"Oh?" Suddenly, he felt scared. She sounded serious.

What would he do if she said she was going to marry Rousseau and move away from Houston?

He listened in shock as she told him about her call from the agency in Los Angeles.

"The woman said this is the opportunity of a lifetime," she finished. "What do you think? Did I do the right thing by taking the job?"

Simon's mind spun. "What does Rousseau have to say about it?"

"I didn't ask Philippe. I'm asking you." Her dark eyes held an odd expression.

How could Simon tell her he didn't want her to take the job? Jenny didn't owe him anything. What could he say, anyway? *Don't go? I'll miss you too much?*

Is that what Jenny would do if the shoe were on the other foot? Lord, the money alone was enough reason for her to say yes.

Simon thought about how Jenny had always been a completely unselfish friend. And that agency woman was right. This *was* the opportunity of a lifetime. "You really loved doing the Hill Country Wine commercials, didn't you?" he finally said.

"Yes," she admitted. "But..."

"But what?"

She shrugged. "Nothing. Yes, I loved doing the commercials. In fact, I was surprised at how much I enjoyed the work. I never expected to."

Simon nodded. His heart felt heavier and heavier. Yet, in fairness, he pushed on. "And the money you would earn doing the swimwear ads would go a long way toward helping you reach your goals, wouldn't it?"

"Yes, it would."

"You would only be gone about a month."

"That's true."

But would she? he wondered. Wasn't it more likely that after this job was over, she'd be offered another job? Then another? Wasn't this just the beginning of a new career for her? One that would take her far away from Houston for long periods of time? One that would introduce her to a different way of life? A life that she was already evincing a fondness for?

More than anything, he wanted to tell her not to go.

More than anything, he wanted her to stay in Houston.

More than anything, he wanted their friendship back.

He wanted Jenny back.

"I think you did the right thing," he said.

Chapter Thirteen

Jenny stared at him.

It was very quiet in the kitchen. Nothing stirred, not even her cats. From outside, she could hear the faint buzz of cicadas. Inside, only the humming refrigerator broke the silence.

All kinds of thoughts tumbled through her mind. It was all she could do not to start crying right then and there.

She'd gambled.

And she'd lost.

She'd been so sure, when he'd walked in tonight, that things were going to be all right. She'd just known he would tell her not to go.

He'd been so sweet tonight. So caring. He'd almost acted like the old Simon. They'd been relaxed together. Their talk had been easy.

All he would have had to do was give her some sign. Anything. Just some small indication that he didn't want her to leave.

But he hadn't.

She had to face it.

He didn't care.

Oh, he *cared*. He loved her as a friend. But he did not care the same way she cared. Those physical reactions he'd had during the filming of the commercials were just that. The reactions of a normal man getting turned on by sexy kisses. She'd been kidding herself thinking he was jealous. All along, he'd probably just been disgusted with her because she wasn't acting like herself. Because she was flirting and acting like one of the women she'd disdained for so long.

Yes, of course, that's exactly what it had been.

The knowledge that he didn't love her lay like a heavy hand upon her heart. She knew that later, after he was gone, she would feel the full thrust of his rejection, but now she had to fight against losing control in front of him. Above all, she couldn't bear the thought that he might feel sorry for her.

They cleaned up the kitchen together, the way they always did. Several times, they brushed against each other while loading the dishwasher. Each time, the band of pain across Jenny's chest tightened and it became harder to breathe. Still, she pretended all was normal.

She had never realized she was this strong. Certainly, she'd told her sister Becky she would be able to handle it if Simon didn't love her. But she wasn't sure she'd really believed it.

She still wasn't sure.

When they'd finished their cleanup, Simon said, "I guess I should be going. It's getting late."

Jenny looked at the wall clock. It was only nine o'clock. She nodded. "Yes. I guess so." *Oh, God, why did it hurt so much? Why did she have to love him this way? Why couldn't she accept that he didn't love her and just get on with it?*

They walked to the front door together.

Hold on. Soon he'll be gone. Just hold on a few more minutes. Then, if you want to go to pieces, you can. You can scream and yell and cry all you want.

Simon reached for the doorknob. With one hand resting on the knob, he turned to her. "When will you be leaving?"

"A week from Friday." The light in the hallway was dim, and Jenny was glad. She was afraid her eyes would give her away. She clenched her fists at her sides. She would not break down. She would not.

He nodded.

Oh, Simon, please say you want me to stay! Please stop looking at me and talking to me as if I were a stranger.

As if he'd divined her thoughts, he reached out to touch her shoulder. A shudder ran through her body. She bit the inside of her lower lip to keep it from trembling and giving her away.

"Jenny..." His voice sounded rough. He leaned forward.

Jenny looked up.

His eyes gleamed in the dusky light.

Slowly, he lowered his head. When his lips touched hers, softly, sweetly, everything in her reached toward him. *Simon, Simon, I love you.*

The kiss only lasted a few seconds.

When he raised his head, he gave her a funny little half smile and said, "Well, if I don't see you before you leave, good luck...with everything."

"Thanks." She gripped the wall next to her as a dizzying wave broke over her.

And then he walked out of her house, taking her heart with him.

Jenny arrived on the island of St. James on a balmy Thursday during the third week of August. Although this was the middle of hurricane season, the production company filming the Sunshine Swimwear ads had decided to risk starting the job now, anyway.

The company had leased a ten-bedroom private villa that sat on a bluff overlooking a secluded cove on the west end of the island. It was owned by a reclusive former movie star who was summering in the Swedish archipelago on the Baltic Sea.

Jenny, who was used to Galveston beaches, couldn't get over the purity and whiteness of the sand or the clear aquamarine depths of the Caribbean. It was a stunningly beautiful setting, one that conjured visions of moonlight swims and romantic evenings.

She was assigned to an airy bedroom that opened onto the wide veranda circling three-quarters of the house. She had arrived in the late afternoon, and after unpacking, she stood at the open window and gazed out at her surroundings.

Moonlight dappled the beach and glistened off the gentle waves, against a backdrop of indigo sky. Stars glittered overhead like thousands of tiny crystals.

The fragrance of lush tropical flowers floated through the soft night air, and in the distance, she could hear the faint strains of calypso music.

She'd been right. St. James was the perfect place for lovers.

Yet here she was, alone and lonely.

Oh, Simon. I miss you so.

All of the heartache, all of the aching loneliness and unhappiness, came rushing back. She closed her eyes, trying to close out the memories in the process.

In the ten days since she and Simon had parted, she thought she had achieved a measure of calm, but now, in this beautiful and romantic setting, her despair returned full force and threatened to demolish her.

She took a deep breath, fighting against the sorrow and feelings of desolation. She'd already spent an entire week crying, and she didn't want to start up again.

It hurt too much.

Besides, wouldn't she look wonderful tomorrow when they started rehearsals if her eyes were all red and puffy? Wouldn't the director just be thrilled?

She had to learn to get on with her life. A life that would not include Simon.

She wondered if they would ever recapture any portion of their friendship. She wasn't really sure if she wanted them to.

She tried to picture them years from now—Simon married to someone else—perhaps the father of a couple of children, and herself—the good friend, maybe godmother to a daughter of his, still single, because she couldn't imagine herself marrying someone else.

Not feeling the way she felt.

At the picture she'd conjured, a lump formed in her throat and misery threatened to overwhelm her again.

Stop torturing yourself!

Sadly, she turned away from the window and headed for the dining room where a buffet supper awaited the crew.

Gail Terno, who was leaving in the morning, introduced her to Alan Suroyer, the producer, and Matt Cretella, the director. Both men seemed nice. Alan was tall, dark and intense; Matt shorter and more open-faced, with friendly green eyes.

Gail then took Jenny over to meet Isabel Gavin, the Sunshine rep. Jenny immediately liked the older woman, who had a no-nonsense look about her and intensely serious dark eyes.

"We're all delighted that you will be the new Sunshine model," Isabel said. "Miss Calvin is especially pleased."

"I'm thrilled to have been asked," Jenny said.

They chatted for a while longer, then Gail led Jenny around to introduce her to the remainder of the crew—makeup, wardrobe, camera and dozens of others. By the time Gail was finished with introductions, everyone ended up being a jumble in Jenny's mind.

She knew that eventually she'd get them all straightened out, but tonight she didn't even try.

About ten o'clock, Alan said, "Rehearsal at eight tomorrow morning. Jenny, report to makeup by six."

Jenny decided with such an early call, she'd better go to bed. Otherwise, she'd have circles under her eyes tomorrow.

Unfortunately, she couldn't fall asleep.

The gentle rhythm of the waves, the distant mating call of some exotic night bird, the wash of moonlight across the wooden floor—sounds and sights that would ordinarily lull her into sleep—all conspired to keep her wide-eyed and thinking of Simon.

She imagined what it would be like to have him here with her, sharing her wide bed with its cool cotton sheets, and tears filled her eyes.

She stirred restlessly, her body achingly empty.

He wasn't ever going to be here.

She had to stop thinking this way.

Who would ever have imagined that she would be here, herself? Only a few months ago, she'd been plain old Jenny Randall, senior editor of a small newspaper, and best friend to Simon Christopher.

Now she was Jenny Randall, actress and model, on location on a gorgeous Caribbean island, and her friendship with Simon Christopher had been relegated to the memory of happier days.

When she finally fell asleep, about two o'clock, she dreamed. Sensuous dreams. Dreams filled with Simon. A Simon who murmured endearments and stroked and caressed her bare skin under a hot sun. A Simon who kissed her deeply, lushly, trailing his lips over her heated body and causing her heart to pound and her insides to melt. A Simon who filled her heart and her body with joy and passion.

So, the next morning, when the alarm went off at five o'clock, Jenny felt sluggish from lack of sleep and sadly bereft from the remnants of her dream. She wanted nothing more than to bury her head under her damp pillow and stay there, hidden from all eyes, for the rest of the day.

Actually, she wished she could hide for the rest of her life.

Coward. Get up. Life goes on.

She dragged herself into the shower, turning the taps on full force.

At six, when she reported to makeup, which had been set up in the kitchen, she felt marginally better.

She also felt determined.

She must stop mooning about.

She must put Simon out of her mind.

She must do this assignment and do it well. Then she would collect her ridiculously large fee, and after that, she would try to decide how she would live the rest of her life.

"What's wrong, Jenny?" Matt Cretella asked.

Jenny walked through the gentle surf to the beach where he stood, megaphone in hand, dressed in neon orange shorts, an L.A. Lakers T-shirt and well-worn sandals. A white sun visor obscured the expression in his green eyes.

It was their first day of rehearsal, and things were not going well. No matter how hard Jenny tried, even she knew something was lacking in her performance.

"Something's bothering you, isn't it?" he said gently. "Do you want to tell me what is?"

"Matt, I'm sorry. I'll do better next time. I promise."

"But Jenny, this is the eleventh time we've run through this part," he said, his voice still gentle. "And you just don't seem to have a lot of life in you."

Jenny swallowed. "I know. Let's do it again. It'll be better. Really." She *would* do this right. She would!

"I don't understand," he continued in a mystified voice. "I've seen your Hill Country commercial, and you were wonderful. Radiant. Incredibly convincing. You're a fantastic actress. What's happened to you?" Some of the frustration he had obviously been trying to hide showed as he fixed her with a bewildered stare.

I'm here under false pretenses, that's what happened! I'm not a fantastic actress. I wasn't acting in those Hill Country commercials. Those feelings I conveyed were real. If Simon were here, if I were acting with him, I'd probably be wonderful again.

Of course she couldn't say any of this.

Now guilt fused with her misery, the weight of it all sapping her of strength. All these people depending on her. All this money already spent transporting them here, renting the villa, getting everything set up.

There was no tomorrow. This was it. She'd made a commitment to these people, and she always honored her commitments. So no matter how miserable she was, she had to get over over it, shape up and get this job done.

Right.

"Dammit," Simon shouted. "Where's the McCandless file?" He charged out of his office.

Cherry jumped as he barreled into the reception area. "Wha-what's wrong?" Her green eyes were as big as half dollars.

"I cannot find the McCandless file," Simon said, firing off each word like individual bullets. "Where is it?" He glared at her. He was sick of her incompetence.

"I—I," she sputtered. "It should be in the middle drawer of your filing cabinet."

"Don't you think I looked there?" Lord, why was he surrounded by stupid people?

Just then, the switchboard buzzed, and Cherry answered. While she talked, she kept darting scared looks Simon's way, which only fueled his anger.

After the call was completed, she removed her headset and said, "I'll go look."

"And leave the switchboard unattended?" he said sarcastically. "Never mind. I'll find it myself."

He stalked off, muttering under his breath.

Ten minutes later, Mark walked into his office. He threw a file down on Simon's desk. "What's wrong with you, Simon?"

Simon picked up the file. The label said Mc-CANDLESS. "Where was it?"

"I had it." Mark plopped into the chair in front of Simon's desk, and gave him a thoughtful perusal. "Why didn't you ask around instead of chewing out Cherry?"

Simon shrugged.

"Are you going to tell me what's eating you?" Mark said.

"Nothing's eating me."

Mark raised his eyebrows. "Oh, come on, Simon. That's hard to believe. You've been charging around here like a bear with a sore paw for nearly two weeks. Everybody's noticed. Hell, everybody's talking about it. Surely you realize the entire staff is trying to stay out of your way. Harriett told me you snapped *her* head off earlier today, and Frank's been avoiding you for days. If you keep on this way, you're going to alienate the entire staff."

Simon sighed. "Sorry."

Mark leaned forward. His expression was earnest, sympathetic. "C'mon, buddy, spill it. This behavior isn't like you. Something's wrong. Maybe I can help."

Simon stared at his partner. His friend. He knew there was a bleakness in his eyes that matched the bleakness in his heart. "I appreciate your offer, Mark, but no one can help what ails me."

Jenny felt desperate.

They were well into their second day of shooting, and so far, they only had about ten seconds of usable film. They needed a lot more. A whole lot more. They were supposed to film three different commercials before leaving. They weren't even close to having enough for one.

On this particular day, they hadn't gotten anything they could use.

And it was all her fault.

Every bit of it was her fault.

She should never have taken this job. It had been a terrible mistake.

She should have known that the only reason she'd been so good in the Hill Country commercials was the fact that she was playing opposite Simon.

What was she going to do?

What was he going to do?

Simon pounded around the track, sweat pouring down his face and into his eyes, blinding him.

Last night, he'd spent the most miserable night of his entire life. He'd hardly slept.

All night long, he'd thought about Jenny.

Over and over, memories of things they'd done together played in his mind.

Her smile—the smile he loved so much—haunted him.

Finally, about four o'clock, he admitted something to himself. Something he had been denying subconsciously, something that should have been obvious to him long, long ago.

He was in love with Jenny.

That was why he had this pain that felt like a huge fireball sitting right in the middle of his chest. That was why he'd been biting everyone's heads off. That was why he was so unhappy.

And so lonely.

He loved her.

Now everything made sense.

He'd probably always been in love with her, and had just never realized it.

He thought about how he felt when Jenny entered a room. How the sight of her always brought a smile to his face. How her appearance was like the sun suddenly showing up on a cloudy, cold day.

He thought about how she was the first person he called when he had good news to share. He thought about how she was the first person he called when he had bad news and needed a sympathetic shoulder.

He thought about how being in her company always made him feel better. How she always listened. How she always had something to contribute.

He thought about how much fun it was to argue with her and how he loved to hear her laugh.

He thought about how he enjoyed teasing her and seeing her eyes light up with mischief as she teased him back.

He thought about how he'd felt when he was kissing her and holding her during the filming of their commercials.

He'd attributed all those feelings to lust. To being horny.

God, he'd been dense!

Of course, he was in love with her.

He must have been completely blind not to have seen it before now.

As he began the cool-down portion of his run, he remembered how he'd asked her to help him figure out what he was doing wrong when it came to finding a woman to marry.

What had she been thinking?

Was it too late for him to find out?

"Let's break for the day," Matt said. "We're not getting anywhere." His look was speculative as Jenny sloshed through the surf.

She knew he was thoroughly and completely baffled by her awful performance so far. She walked up to him and waited until he concluded a conversation with Tiffany, his assistant.

When Tiffany, after shooting Jenny a commiserating look, walked off, Jenny said, "Matt, I'm sorry."

He nodded. Then he sighed and squeezed her shoulder. "Jenny, if things don't improve soon, I'm going to have to replace you. You know that, don't you?''

That night, Jenny couldn't sleep.

She'd lost her job at the paper.

She'd lost Simon.

And now it looked as if she was going to lose this job, too.

She would have nothing left.

Simon went into the office only long enough to tell Mark what he'd decided to do.

Then he picked up the phone and called Emma Goodman.

"Simon!" she said. "What a surprise!" Then a note of alarm crept into her voice. "Is Jenny all right?"

"Jenny's fine. At least, as far as I know. I haven't talked to her since she went down to the Caribbean."

"That's a relief."

"How's everything going with you?"

"Oh, well, you know...it's hard to be idle after you've worked for so many years." Her voice sounded wistful. "It's also hard not to be a part of something you helped build."

"So you haven't managed to completely fill up your days yet, huh?" Simon said.

"Oh, don't go feeling sorry for me. I'm fine. I just miss being out every day. I never was much for bingo and such."

Simon smiled. "In that case, I've got a proposition for you. How would you like to come to work for me here at the agency?"

"Simon! Me? Why, what would I do?"

"The same thing you did at the *Vanguard*. Keep the books and run the office. We can use the extra help. We've been meaning to hire someone for a while, and today I talked to my partner and told him about you, and he agreed that I should call you."

He felt better than he'd felt in days, weeks, even, when he hung up after extracting her promise that she would report to the office first thing in the morning.

Next, he called his travel agent.

An hour later, she called back. "I've got you booked on an eight-o'clock flight to Miami tomorrow morning."

For the rest of the day, Simon took care of everything that needed doing: he took his dog to the vet's for boarding, he asked his across-the-street neighbor to pick up his mail, he called and stopped the newspaper delivery, he cleaned out the refrigerator and he went to the bank and withdrew some money.

Then he hit Banana Republic, where he bought himself some new shorts and cotton shirts and a wide-brimmed hat. His last stop was his favorite shoe store, where he purchased a pair of brown leather sandals.

He grinned.

He hadn't worn sandals since he was a kid. They felt good. He wiggled his toes experimentally. They felt damned good. Maybe he would stay in the islands and be a beach bum for the rest of his life.

That night, he spent his second nearly sleepless night, but this time he couldn't sleep because of the excitement churning in this gut.

Tomorrow he would be in St. James.

Tomorrow he would see Jenny.

God, he hoped it wasn't too late.

* * *

He arrived at the Seaside Inn in downtown St. James at exactly four twenty-five the next afternoon. His travel agent had booked him a private cabana. It took him less than thirty minutes to check in, unpack, shed his stateside clothes and put on a pair of white shorts, a pale blue knit shirt and his sandals.

He hadn't tried to find out where Jenny was staying before leaving Houston. He could have called her mother or her sister Becky, but he hadn't wanted them to know what he was doing.

What if Jenny told him to go suck lemons? After the stupid way he'd behaved, he wouldn't blame her if she did. Anyway, Simon figured the island was so small, a production company and film crew wouldn't be difficult to locate. People were bound to know where they were filming.

On his first try, he hit pay dirt.

A smiling bartender at the hotel bar, who insisted Simon call him Ernest—"You know, like in Ernest Hemingway"—told him the crew was filming out on the west end of the island. "They are living in Greta Bergstedt's home," he said in his soft island patois. "The crew, they have been coming here to drink and dance at night," he added.

Simon had a sudden vivid picture of Jenny dressed in some kind of flowered skirt and off-the-shoulder blouse, dancing with a handsome cameraman or good-looking grip. Jealousy knifed through him.

What had he been thinking of, letting her go? Had he been crazy? She'd been down here in this romantic paradise for days already!

He thanked Ernest and went out to find a taxi. A young, skinny, very loquacious kid of about seventeen, driving a Jeep painted bright yellow, drove Simon out to the Bergstedt place.

They bumped over a sandy two-lane road that paralleled the sea on the left. Dunes dotted with tropical vegetation marked their route on the right. As they left the town, the homes became bigger and more ostentatious.

"Lots of rich people, they live here, man," said the driver, who'd introduced himself as Mickey. "Are you rich, too?"

Simon smiled. "No, I'm not rich."

"I think you are. All Americans are rich." Mickey's dark eyes gleamed.

Simon decided he wouldn't burst Mickey's bubble. He would give him a generous tip.

"We almost there," Mickey said. He pointed to a bluff in the distance. "That house is the one you want, man."

Simon saw a huge sand-colored villa with a red tile roof and a shaded veranda. The house was surrounded by flowering white shrubs of a kind he didn't recognize and scarlet and purple bougainvillea.

His heart kicked into high gear.

Soon.

Soon he would see Jenny.

He just hoped she would be glad to see him.

A few minutes later, he paid Mickey, adding a ridiculously big tip, thanked him and climbed out of the Jeep. He looked around. The house looked deserted.

He walked closer, until he'd crested the bluff.

It was then he saw the film crew.

They were scattered like ants over the beach below. Cameras, cables, boxes of equipment, tents, peo-

ple—they dotted the beach with the paraphernalia of
their craft.

He lifted his sunglasses and scanned the scene.

Where was Jenny?

And then he saw her.

She stood in the surf, shading her eyes, looking in
the direction of a man Simon guessed must be the director. He was saying something to her, and she was
nodding.

Jenny. Jenny. Simon's pulse quickened.

She turned, walking farther out into the water. Her
shoulders seemed to slump, and there was something
about her demeanor that looked dejected.

Simon's heart was beating too fast. He clambered
down the slope of the dune, avoiding stray rocks and
clumps of grass. The sand felt warm as it oozed between his toes. The sun on the water was so bright, it
hurt his eyes to look at it. He stopped at the perimeter
of the beach. It looked as if they were beginning to
film, and he didn't want to interfere.

Jenny stood about twenty feet out. She was tanned,
more tanned than Simon had ever seen her. She wore
a white maillot cut in a deep V in front and high on her
hips. She looked incredibly sexy. Incredibly beautiful. Simon wanted to take off his shoes and run out
into the water and scoop her up into his arms.

He wanted to kiss her senseless.

He wanted to make mad, passionate love to her and
never let her up for air.

He forced himself to remain still.

The director raised his megaphone, and the crew fell
silent.

"Okay, Jenny," the director shouted. "Now run through the surf, and let's see some *joy* in your face! Pretend you're running toward your lover, and you haven't seen him for a long time. Pretend you're happier than you've ever been because he's here. Can you do that for me?"

Simon frowned. The director sounded irritated with her. What was his problem?

"Action!" the director called.

The cameras began rolling.

Jenny began running, water splashing up around her.

"Cut!" yelled the director. He yanked off his sun visor. "It's no good. No good."

Jenny hung her head. She looked as if she was going to cry.

Simon couldn't stand it. He walked forward. Curious crew members stared at him as he threaded his way through the equipment. When he reached the edge of the beach, he shouted, "Jenny!"

She looked up.

For a moment, she looked bewildered. Then, in a blinding burst, a radiant smile appeared. "Simon!"

She ran toward him, laughing.

"Yes!" the director yelled. "That's it! That's it! Roll those cameras! That's *exactly* the expression I wanted!"

Chapter Fourteen

For one impossibly long moment, she was afraid to believe. She squeezed her eyes shut, her heart going haywire in her chest.

Please, God, don't let it be a dream.

She opened her eyes again.

It was no dream.

Simon still stood there, waving and grinning and looking fantastic.

Laughing, she raced through the surf, hardly hearing Matt Cretella yelling through the megaphone.

Her feet hit the sand, and she hurled herself into Simon's arms. "Simon, Simon," she said. "Where did you come from? Oh, I'm so glad to see you!"

"Jenny!"

And then he kissed her. A heart-stopping, earth-shattering, turn-your-knees-to-jelly kiss that lifted her right off the planet Earth and shot her into orbit.

Jenny's heart soared with the most indescribable happiness as she wound her arms around him and gave herself up to his kiss.

When he finally released her, and she settled back down to earth, she realized that she'd given no thought to why he was there or the fact that they were surrounded by dozens of curious people.

"Oh, I've gotten you all wet," she said, ineffectually trying to brush sand off of him. She knew she was grinning like a fool.

"It doesn't matter."

"What are you *doing* here? You nearly gave me heart failure, I was so shocked when I saw you."

He looked around. "Uh, could we go somewhere and talk privately for a few minutes?"

"All right, people, why don't we take five?" Matt Cretella said.

He'd been standing only a few feet away the whole time, Jenny realized. Suddenly, she felt embarrassed by her complete disregard for her surroundings and the way she'd practically thrown herself at Simon. What must they all think? She met Matt's gaze, but he only grinned and winked.

The crew scattered.

Simon grabbed her hand and led her down the beach and around a curve, out of sight of curious eyes. Then he slid his arms around her and kissed her once more—a long greedy kiss that got her heart pounding again. His hands cupped her bottom, molding her to him, and desire throbbed deep inside of her.

The hot sun beat down.

The waves lapped the shore.

Birds flew overhead.

And Jenny and Simon kissed as if they would never get enough of each other.

"Jenny, Jenny," he muttered against her ear, "I missed you so much. I couldn't stand it. I had to come." His breathing sounded ragged.

"Oh, Simon, I missed you, too," she cried. She still stood plastered up against him, and through the thin fabric of her wet swimsuit, she felt every line of his body, every evidence of the desire he felt for her. Her own body pulsed in response as he held her fast.

He kissed her cheeks and her eyes and the tip of her nose. "I've been so blind. I can't believe it took me this long to realize that I was in love with you." He looked deep into her eyes. "All these years. You've always been there. My best friend. And now... now I realize how dense I've been. When you left, I felt as if the bottom had dropped out of my world. I love you so much, Jenny."

Jenny smiled tearfully. He loved her! The knowledge vibrated through her. She had waited so long to hear those words. So very long.

"I love you, too," she whispered. Her heart was so full, she could hardly speak. "I've loved you for so long. And I thought it was hopeless."

He smiled tenderly. "Jenny, sweetheart, why are you crying?"

Only then did she realize that she *was* crying. She sniffed. "Because I'm so happy."

"Silly goose," he said. He kissed her again—a slow sweet kiss full of the promise of kisses yet to come. "It might have taken me a while to realize the obvious, but

I'm not really stupid, you know. I was bound to figure it out sooner or later.''

She laughed, swiping at her tears and thinking that maybe she should pinch herself to be sure this was real. "You almost waited too long," she teased. "I was about to run off with a tour guide."

He smiled—that slow sexy smile she loved so much. "A tour guide, huh? Where is he? I'll punch out his lights."

The most delicious sense of well-being snaked through her. "Would you really?"

Simon grinned. "Try me. I nearly punched out Rousseau's lights a couple of times."

"So you really *were* jealous?" Jenny said in delight.

"I was sick with jealousy, but I couldn't admit it. I kept telling myself I was mad at you for falling for his lines."

Jenny gave him a mock frown. "Now Simon—"

"C'mon. You gotta admit it. You *were* flirting and batting your eyes a lot."

"I was just trying to get your attention."

"You've got it now, sweetheart."

Just then, Matt Cretella called through his megaphone. "Break's over. Let's get back to work!"

Jenny started guiltily. "Simon, I've got to go."

He tipped her chin up. "Okay. But kiss me first."

A few minutes later, after they'd walked back to where the rest of the crew was gathered, Matt looked at Simon and said, "Hi. I'm Matt Cretella, the director."

"Simon Christopher."

The two men shook hands and sized each other up.

Jenny felt so proud as she watched Simon. Oh, she loved him! She'd gotten such a rush when she'd seen him on the beach. She wondered how long he planned to stay. She wondered what his coming here meant. He'd said he loved her, but what did that *mean?*

She knew that none of her questions would be answered immediately.

"I hope you're gonna stick around," Matt said. "You seem to be good for Jenny."

Simon smiled, eyeing Jenny. "Wild horses couldn't drag me away."

The rest of the shoot went wonderfully. Jenny was so ecstatically happy, she couldn't stop smiling.

Matt was delighted.

They shot roll after roll of film, until the sun began to lower, and the light changed.

"That's it for today," Matt said reluctantly. He looked at Simon. "You gonna be here tomorrow?"

"Like I said, wild horses couldn't drag me away."

Simon accompanied Jenny to the house. He waited on the veranda, a cool drink in his hand, while she showered and changed for the evening. He'd told her to put on a dress.

"I'm taking you out for dinner, then we're going to go dancing and after that..." His voice trailed off.

"After that," he continued, his voice husky, "it's up to you." He cleared his throat. "But you might want to pack an overnight bag."

Jenny shivered at the look in his eyes.

She dressed carefully but quickly. She couldn't stand being away from Simon any longer than absolutely necessary. She'd already been away from him too long.

She had purchased a sea green sundress before she left Houston, and now, with her tan, it looked really good, she thought, slipping it over her shoulders and zipping it up. Strappy white sandals, and green-and-white striped button earrings with matching chunky bracelets completed her outfit.

She spritzed herself with her favorite perfume, fluffed up her hair and sprayed it, and hastily stuffed clean underwear, a short pink nightie, a few toiletries, and shorts and a T-shirt into a large canvas tote bag.

Her face heated as she realized exactly what she was doing, and a quivering anticipation danced in her belly.

Five minutes later, tote bag in hand, she walked outside.

Simon's heart thudded up into his throat when Jenny walked out onto the veranda. The setting sun gilded her, and in her sea-colored dress, she reminded him of a water nymph—all fresh and lovely and graceful.

He ached to touch her.

He ached to kiss her.

He ached to make love to her.

Desire, like a giant fist, clutched at him, and suddenly Simon found it hard to breathe. He wanted to throw her to the ground and ravish her on the spot. But he would tamp down his caveman instincts... for now. Because he wanted tonight to be special. A night they would remember all of their lives.

Tonight, he intended to take it slow. Very slow.

She smiled as she drew nearer.

He feasted his eyes on her. How could he not love her?

She was the sweetest, the nicest, the most warm and wonderful woman in the world.

She was also unbelievably sexy and desirable.

A fierce possessiveness filled him as his gaze slid to the tote and he knew, without any doubt, that she wanted the exact thing he wanted.

The way he was looking at her caused her heart to beat faster. Shyness threatened her, especially when his gaze moved to the big tote she carried.

The knowledge that they would make love tonight thrummed between them like a current of electricity.

Jenny's mouth suddenly felt dry. Her heartbeat sounded too loud, and she was sure he could hear it.

She licked her lips.

His eyes followed the movement.

Something hot coiled deep within.

They stood there like that, motionless, while their bodies called to each other and their eyes devoured each other and their thoughts centered on the realization that tonight they would not deny their feelings.

Tonight, they would fulfill their destiny.

Tonight, they would become lovers.

Later, as they sat hand in hand in the back seat of a taxi with the windows open to the balmy tropical night, Jenny thought about how she'd never really believed this would happen.

Simon gave the driver the address of his hotel. "I need to change, and you need to dump that bag," he explained, squeezing her hand.

They arrived at the Seaside Inn in less than fifteen minutes. Simon tipped the driver generously, then grabbed her hand again and led her down a winding path bordered with flowers to his private cabana.

Jenny was relieved to see that he had a separate living room and she would not have to sit in the bedroom while he changed clothes. Even though she loved him, and even though she wanted him, there was something very intimate about watching a person dress and undress. She wasn't quite ready. The changes in their relationship were coming about too fast; her mind hadn't had time to get adjusted to them, but later... The thought trailed off, causing butterflies to start up in her stomach.

She settled onto a comfortable flower-cushioned wicker sofa while Simon disappeared into his bedroom.

She noticed he left the door open.

Within minutes, she heard the sound of a shower. She plucked a copy of *People* magazine from the glass-topped coffee table and leafed through it, but her mind kept wandering. She couldn't stop picturing Simon in the shower, the water sluicing his firm body.

She closed her eyes.

Jenny had a fantasy.

Her fantasy involved taking a bath with Simon. She remembered a movie she'd seen years ago where the heroine lit dozens of candles and then she and the hero took a bath together, the candles flickering around them. It had been one of the most sensuous, seductive scenes imaginable, probably because it seemed so deliciously forbidden.

Jenny had thought about that scene so many times. And in her imagination, it was her with Simon in that tub.

The water stopped.

Jenny tried to stop thinking about that bathtub. Perhaps there wasn't even a bathtub here.

She pretended to be absorbed in her magazine when Simon emerged about ten minutes later.

Her heart caught in her throat.

Oh, she loved to look at him.

He was wearing loose white cotton pants and an open-necked dark blue shirt. On his feet were white Topsiders. He grinned, his dimples cutting deep grooves in his cheeks. "Ready?" he said.

Jenny stood. "Ready."

They walked out into the soft night. Simon slipped his arm around her waist, and Jenny caught a whiff of his after-shave, or maybe it was his cologne. The smell, crisp and lemony, did something to her.

She loved the way he smelled.

They walked slowly down the path toward the lights of the main building.

"I thought we would have dinner here," he said. "I noticed they have an outdoor patio."

"Okay."

The smiling hostess seated them on the patio where colored lanterns bobbed in the breeze and a small combo played lilting island music. Candles sputtered on the tables, and all around them, soft laughter wafted through the air.

Jenny thought it was the most romantic place she'd ever seen.

Everything about the evening took on a dreamlike quality. The food was luscious—some kind of chicken baked in wine, served with rice and vegetables and rich, buttery rolls. Simon chose a crisp white wine to accompany the meal. "Sorry, no Hill Country," he said laughingly.

Afterward, Jenny never remembered eating or drinking. All she remembered was looking at Simon, listening to his familiar voice, seeing his familiar smile, yet feeling as if everything about him was new and excitingly different.

After a tart lemon custard dessert and coffee, Simon stood and reached for her hand. He led her to the dance floor, and even though Jenny protested that she didn't know how to dance to this kind of music, Simon wouldn't hear her excuses.

"We'll fake it," he said, smiling down into her eyes. "All we have to do is sway."

And that's what they did. Standing close together, her arms around his neck, his around her waist, they swayed to the happy music and looked into each other's eyes and each thought about what would come later.

When the candles had burned low, and the patio began to empty as couple after couple sauntered off, Simon pulled her closer, and murmured against her ear. "Jenny...I want to make love to you."

Jenny's heart skittered. She closed her eyes. A thrill of anticipation shimmered through her, and her skin suddenly felt too tight for her body.

"Do you want that, too?" he whispered. He kissed her ear, letting his tongue trace the inside.

Jenny shuddered. Her arms tightened around him as she pressed closer. "Yes," she whispered. "Yes, that's what I want more than anything in the world."

Jenny knew she would never forget this night.

If she lived to be one hundred years old, this night would remain as clear and bright as the finest diamond.

They walked slowly back to Simon's cabana. Several times they stopped to kiss. Each kiss only heightened Jenny's awareness and her delicious sense of anticipation.

When they reached the cabana, Simon turned on one lamp, and a soft golden glow illuminated the living room.

He took her hand and drew her slowly into his arms. Jenny sighed as their lips met. He kissed her gently, grazing her lips with his. They kissed again and again, and each time, each kiss became longer and more involved.

More insistent.

More demanding.

Simon's tongue drove deep into her mouth, and his hands splayed across her bottom, urging her closer. She felt his heat against her, felt how much he wanted her, and an answering want spiraled down, into the very core of her.

Gradually, between kisses, they moved slowly into the bedroom. The windows were open and moonlight spilled into the room, giving it a pearlescent glow. A fan whirred slowly overhead. Jenny noticed that the bed was already turned down. She also noticed it wasn't a very big bed, and her pulse hammered.

They undressed each other.

Simon's hands trembled as he unzipped her dress and helped her lift it off.

Jenny had an attack of shyness as he looked at her standing there clad only in her filmy bra and panties.

"You're so beautiful," he whispered, touching her.

She arched toward him. She had dreamed of this moment so many times. But the reality was better than her dreams. Infinitely better. She allowed herself to enjoy his touch, and then, unable to resist, she touched him, too.

He gasped.

Then hurriedly, he shed his own clothes, and she helped him, her shyness a thing of the past. This was Simon, after all, and she had loved him for a long, long time.

Before long, all the barriers between them were gone.

He lifted her and held her close for a moment. They gazed into each other's eyes. "You're sure?" he whispered.

"I've never been more sure of anything in my entire life," she said.

He smiled and carried her to the bed.

Jenny hadn't thought she could love Simon any more than she did already, but throughout that night, her love grew even stronger.

He was such a thoughtful lover.

Tender and caring.

His slow kisses and slow hands skimmed over her body, making her feel loved and special and oh so desirable.

She responded in kind.

She loved touching him, she discovered. She learned things about him that she'd never known. How if she caressed him in a certain spot, he would tremble under her fingertips. How if she kissed in a certain way, he would moan deep in his throat.

He was such a generous lover.

He seemed to care only for her pleasure, not his own.

"Do you like that?" he asked, over and over again.

"Oh, yes. I like that," Jenny responded.

He was such a romantic lover.

He told her again and again how beautiful she was and how much he loved her.

And when he finally raised himself over her, spreading her legs and entering her slowly, Jenny's life became complete. Jenny became complete. She finally understood exactly what all the songs and all the books and all the myths were about.

This man belonged to her.

And she belonged to him.

The physical union, the mating of their bodies, the joy and exquisite pleasure they gave each other, completed the circle that had begun with their friendship.

She drew him in, and held him close, and felt his life force spill into her body, and her own body soared in answer.

Afterward, they lay entwined for a long time. Replete. Happy. Warmly contented.

He kissed her lazily, tracing his fingers over her collarbone, trailing them down to touch one breast, then another. "I love your breasts," he whispered.

Jenny smiled. So happy. She was so happy. "They're kind of small, don't you think?"

"They're perfect." He kissed them, first one, then the other. "I love the way the little nipples pop up. Just like little grapes. Mmm, sweet," he said.

Jenny blushed. She was glad it was dark, because she knew Simon would tease her if he could see her red face.

"Stop blushing," he said, continuing to nuzzle her nipples. "I always did love grapes...."

She pushed at him, but he just laughed and continued playing with her.

So he was a playful lover, too.

He was perfect, she thought. Absolutely, completely, undeniably perfect.

They made love again.

And later, yet again.

"Don't you ever get tired?" she asked.

"Of this? Never."

She smiled happily.

Finally, they slept.

When Jenny awoke, she was lying in the warm circle of Simon's arms, her back against his front, fitted together like two pieces of a jigsaw puzzle. One of his hands cupped her breast, the other lay flat against her stomach.

She wished she could stay this way forever.

Unfortunately, she was a working girl. And she could see the sun coming up, its silvery pink light creeping over the horizon. And she had an early makeup call.

She stirred.

Simon awoke slowly.

She decided he looked so cute in the morning, with his hair all tousled and his eyes all clouded and sleepy and stubble on his chin.

"Where you goin', woman?" he said thickly, reaching for her as she tried to extricate herself.

"I have to go to work, remember?"

He frowned. "Phooey."

She grinned.

"Gimme one kiss first," he wheedled.

"Uh-uh. I know you. You won't be satisfied with one kiss."

His sleepy eyes turned mischievous. "That's the trouble with making out with your best friend. She knows you too well."

She chuckled. "Is that what we did last night? Make out?"

"Among other things." He grabbed her hand, yanking her back to him. He rolled on top of her, then kissed her hard. "I love you," he said gruffly. "And don't you forget it."

As if she could forget it.

His words, his eyes, his touch, his lovemaking, the way he made her feel, were all she could think about.

Throughout the rest of that day, while she worked, she thought about him.

Matt was ecstatic. "You look radiant," he said. His eyes slid to Simon, sitting at the perimeter of the crew.

Jenny was too happy to blush.

"How long are you staying?" Jenny asked that night as they lay in his bed, sated after making love.

"I may never leave," Simon murmured. He kissed her nose. "It's too much fun here."

"Seriously..."

"How long will the filming last?"

"Another week or two, depending on how things go."

"Then I'll stay another week or two."

Jenny smiled.

"Do you have any fantasies?" Jenny asked later.

"You're fulfilling all of them," he said.

"I have a fantasy," Jenny said.

It was their third night together.

"Oh? What?"

She told him about the movie she remembered.

He smiled. "That was *Bull Durham*. I remember that scene, too." He kissed her ear. "Sorry that I don't have a tub."

The next day, when Jenny finished filming, Simon said he had to go back to his room and that she should go to hers and get ready for the evening.

"I'll pick you up in an hour and a half," he promised, a secretive glint in his eyes.

Jenny wondered what he was up to. Then she giggled. Actually, she knew full well what he was normally up to.

"Where are we going?" Jenny asked curiously. "This isn't your cabana."

He smiled slowly. "It is now."

When they got inside the new cabana, he led her to the bathroom.

Jenny gasped.

In the center of the bathroom stood a huge, oval tub. All around it were dozens of candles, just waiting to be lit.

If she could have loved Simon more, she would have.

Later, she thought about how sometimes fantasies were so much better than the reality.

This time, the reality exceeded even her imaginings.

The heated water, the scented bath oil, the flickering candles, the soft music playing on the radio.

Jenny thought she'd died and gone to heaven.

"Are you happy now?" Simon whispered after her shuddering body collapsed against him.

"I'm not sure," she said as her breathing finally began to slow. "We might have to try that again before I'll be certain."

"Your wish is my command," Simon said just before his mouth closed over hers.

There was only one fly in the ointment.

As the days flew by, Simon said nothing about their future.

He said he loved her, hundreds of times.

But he never said he wanted to marry her.

As day after day passed, Jenny started to worry.

Why hadn't he said anything?

What was he thinking?

* * *

Simon watched the filming, regret consuming him. This was the crew's last day. Gail Terno, who had returned to St. James yesterday, watched with him.

"She's fabulous," Gail said.

"Yes, she is," Simon agreed. God, he loved her. He couldn't believe how many years he'd wasted.

"She's got a fantastic future, if she wants it," Gail said.

"I know." That's why he felt such regret. Now decisions would have to be made. Their idyll would soon be over and real life would step in.

He wanted to marry Jenny.

He wanted her to come home to Houston with him, marry him and stay there.

But how could he ask her to give this up?

He could see that she loved it.

And she was wonderful.

He wondered if he could be happy traipsing around the world with her. He considered it. He could sell his half of the agency to Mark. And if that was the only way he could have Jenny, he wouldn't mind. But how long could he be happy being Mr. Jenny Randall? With no identity of his own and no productive work to do?

These two weeks had been fun. They'd been incredible, actually. But he'd always known they would have to end.

Like Jenny's bathtub fantasy—he smiled, remembering—St. James was fantasyland.

And he and Jenny were flesh-and-blood human beings who needed to work as well as play.

He frowned.

What if he didn't sell the business? What if he simply stayed in Houston when Jenny had to travel? Could that work? Could they build any kind of committed relationship that way?

He didn't see how. He wanted a family. Children. And he thought Jenny did, too. She used to, anyway.

What kind of life would that be? Jenny gone half the time. Maybe more than half the time.

It was really ironic.

Jenny was now exactly the kind of person he used to encourage her to be. And he was more the kind of person she had been before.

"I've got another client who's interested in Jenny," Gail said, breaking into his thoughts. "It's print work, and we'll shoot in London and then in Paris."

Simon looked at her. What was she trying to tell him? Not to stand in Jenny's way?

For the rest of the day, he couldn't get the woman's words out of his mind.

Matt Cretella invited the entire crew to be his guests for dinner at the elegant Hyatt Regency's rooftop restaurant. "To celebrate," he said.

Jenny wore the sexy black dress she'd worn for one of the Hill Country Wine commercials.

Simon wore a dark suit and white shirt and red tie.

"I thought you said you didn't bring a suit," Jenny said.

He smiled. "I didn't. I bought this one at some ridiculously expensive tourist trap."

The evening was bittersweet for Jenny.

Tomorrow they would all leave St. James.

The place where she had become a complete woman.

The place where she had been happier than she'd ever been in her entire life.

The evening was bittersweet for Simon.

He wished he could keep Jenny here, in his arms, for the rest of his life.

He wanted to hold tomorrow off.

Forever.

Jenny listened incredulously as Gail Terno told her about the new assignment she had in mind. "Forever Young Makeup wants me?"

"Yes," Gail said happily. "I told them you would probably want at least a week or two to rest up. They agreed that the first week in October should be perfect for what they have in mind."

She went on to describe shots in front of Buckingham Palace with the palace guard in the background, one by Big Ben, another in Piccadilly Circus. "And when we're in Paris, there's the Eiffel Tower, Notre Dame, sidewalk cafés. Oh, it's going to be fabulous. Have you ever been to Europe, or will this be your first trip?"

Jenny chewed at her inner lip. Gail talked as if this were a fait accompli. "Listen, Gail..."

"I think you'll get to keep your wardrobe, if you want to," Gail barreled on, ignoring Jenny's attempt to interrupt. "And you know, it might be a good idea for you to get a portfolio done while you're in Houston. I can put you in touch with a great photographer. He does a lot of black-and-white print work."

"Gail, wait. I—I'm not interested."

"You're not *interested!* How could you not be interested? This is a wonderful assignment. Most models would kill for this kind of work."

"I'm not most models. In fact, I'm not even a model. I'm a writer."

Gail rolled her eyes. "You *used* to be a writer. Now you're a top-paid actress and model."

Jenny sighed. "This isn't the way I want to live the rest of my live. I want to go home to Houston, and I want to write."

Later, as she and Simon boarded their plane, Jenny thought about the "missed opportunity" and knew that she would never have regrets.

Even if he never asked her to marry him. Even if these past couple of weeks with Simon were all she ever had, she still would have no regrets.

But, oh, she hoped he would want to marry her. He'd told her months ago he was ready. And he'd said he loved her. What was stopping him from making that commitment?

Once they were airborne, she said, "Gail Terno offered me a job representing Forever Young Makeup."

He nodded, not meeting her eyes. "I know."

"You know?"

"Yes, she told me about it yesterday."

"I see."

Now he looked at her. His blue eyes were clouded. He didn't smile. "How soon will you have to go to London?"

She gazed into those eyes that she'd loved for such a long time. It was all clear to her now. Every bit of it. She smiled. "I turned her down."

She watched as his eyes changed, brightened and filled with happiness. "Why?" he said softly.

"Because I don't want to be a model or an actress. I'm a writer. I want to be in Houston, with you, and I want to pursue the goals I've neglected the past few months."

Their hearts were full as they said with their eyes all the things that couldn't be said in such a public place.

He took her hand and held it tightly as the plane climbed. "I love you," he whispered.

"I love you," she whispered back.

He leaned closer. "Will you marry me, Jenny?"

Her smile was radiant. "It's what I want more than anything in the world."

His eyes turned mischievous. "You said that once before, if I recall."

"It's not very gentlemanly of you to remind me how wanton I can be," she answered.

His smile told her how much he loved her and what a wonderful future they would have together. "I sure do like wanton women," he whispered.

Jenny decided she didn't care how many people were watching them. She pulled his head down, closed her eyes and gave herself up to his kiss.

* * * * *

Silhouette®

SPECIAL EDITION™

COMING NEXT MONTH

#967 A MATCH FOR CELIA—Gina Ferris Wilkins
That Special Woman!/The Family Way

Carefree Celia Carson wanted excitement—and a man to match.
She thought Reed Hollander was like every other man she'd met,
but his mysterious past promised to give her more than she'd
bargained for!

#968 MOTHER AT HEART—Robin Elliott
Man, Woman and Child

Knowing he had no other family to take care of him, Tessa Russell
raised her nephew as her son. Then she found out the identity of
his father—would Dominic Bonelli now want to claim Jason as
his own?

#969 FATHER IN TRAINING—Susan Mallery
Hometown Heartbreakers

Sandy Walker first caught Kyle Haynes's eye back when they
were teenagers. Now she was a single mom and he a swinging
single. Kyle still loved Sandy, but could he promise her forever?

#970 COWBOY'S KISS—Victoria Pade
A Ranching Family

Die-hard cowboy Jackson Heller was not happy about sharing
his land with Ally Brooks and her young daughter. But city girl
Ally was determined to learn ranching, and Jackson soon found
himself falling in love....

#971 HERE TO STAY—Kate Freiman

After losing his memory in an accident, Miles Kent feared his
lost, unknown past. Sasha Reiss wanted to help him rebuild his
life, and to show him that her love was here to stay.

#972 NO KIDS OR DOGS ALLOWED—Jane Gentry

Falling in love was the easy part for Elizabeth Fairchild and
Steve Riker. But their two teenage daughters couldn't stand each
other. With the wedding day coming up, could the marriage go
off without a hitch?

Take 4 bestselling love stories FREE

Plus get a FREE surprise gift!

Special Limited-time Offer

Mail to Silhouette Reader Service™

3010 Walden Avenue
P.O. Box 1867
Buffalo, N.Y. 14269-1867

YES! Please send me 4 free Silhouette Special Edition® novels and my free surprise gift. Then send me 6 brand-new novels every month, which I will receive months before they appear in bookstores. Bill me at the low price of $2.89 each plus 25¢ delivery and applicable sales tax, if any.* That's the complete price and a savings of over 10% off the cover prices—quite a bargain! I understand that accepting the books and gift places me under no obligation ever to buy any books. I can always return a shipment and cancel at any time. Even if I never buy another book from Silhouette, the 4 free books and the surprise gift are mine to keep forever.

235 BPA ANRQ

Name	(PLEASE PRINT)
Address	Apt. No.
City	State	Zip

In June, get ready for thrilling romances and FREE BOOKS—Western-style— with...

WESTERN *Lovers*

You can receive the first 2 Western Lovers titles FREE!

June 1995 brings Harlequin and Silhouette's WESTERN LOVERS series, which combines larger-than-life love stories set in the American West! And WESTERN LOVERS brings you stories with your favorite themes... "Ranch Rogues," "Hitched In Haste," "Ranchin' Dads," "Reunited Hearts" the packaging on each book highlights the popular theme found in each WESTERN LOVERS story!

And in June, when you buy either of the Men Made In America titles, you will receive a WESTERN LOVERS title absolutely FREE! Look for these fabulous combinations:

◆ Buy ALL IN THE FAMILY
by Heather Graham Pozzessere (Men Made In America) and receive a FREE copy of
BETRAYED BY LOVE by Diana Palmer
(Western Lovers)

◆ Buy THE WAITING GAME
by Jayne Ann Krentz (Men Made In America) and receive a FREE copy of
IN A CLASS BY HIMSELF by JoAnn Ross
(Western Lovers)

Look for the special, extra-value shrink-wrapped packages at your favorite retail outlet!

HARLEQUIN®   *Silhouette*®

WL-T

He's Too Hot To Handle...but she can take a little heat.

Announcing
the New Pages & Privileges™ Program
from Harlequin® and Silhouette®

Get All This FREE
With Just One Proof-of-Purchase!

- **FREE Hotel Discounts** of up to 60% off at leading hotels in the U.S., Canada and Europe

- **FREE Travel Service** with the guaranteed lowest available airfares plus 5% cash back on every ticket

- **FREE $25 Travel Voucher** to use on any ticket on any airline booked through our Travel Service

- **FREE Petite Parfumerie** collection (a $50 Retail value)

- **FREE Insider Tips Letter** full of fascinating information and hot sneak previews of upcoming books

- **FREE Mystery Gift** (if you enroll before June 15/95)

And there are more great gifts and benefits to come!
Enroll today and become Privileged!

(see insert for details)

PROOF-OF-PURCHASE

Offer expires October 31, 1996   SSE-PP2